David Boswell Reid, Elisha Harris

Ventilation in American Dwellings

David Boswell Reid, Elisha Harris

Ventilation in American Dwellings

Reprint of the original, first published in 1864.

1st Edition 2022 | ISBN: 978-3-75259-349-5

Verlag (Publisher): Salzwasser Verlag GmbH, Zeilweg 44, 60439 Frankfurt, Deutschland
Vertretungsberechtigt (Authorized to represent): E. Roepke, Zeilweg 44, 60439 Frankfurt, Deutschland
Druck (Print): Books on Demand GmbH, In de Tarpen 42, 22848 Norderstedt, Deutschland

VENTILATION

IN

AMERICAN DWELLINGS;

WITH

A SERIES OF DIAGRAMS,

PRESENTING EXAMPLES IN DIFFERENT
CLASSES OF HABITATIONS.

BY DAVID BOSWELL REID, M.D., F.R.S.E.

TO WHICH IS ADDED

AN INTRODUCTORY OUTLINE OF THE PROGRESS OF IMPROVEMENT IN VENTILATION,

BY ELISHA HARRIS, M.D.

———

NEW YORK

1864.

PREFACE.

THE object of the following pages is to present a series of examples of ventilation applied to American habitations, and to assist in the introduction of more extended measures for meeting cases of extreme temperature, whether of heat or cold.

Some apology may, perhaps, be required on the part of the author, in entering on this subject. There is no practical question, probably, where the experience of different nations can prove more mutually advantageous than in those departments of Art and Science that minister to the wants of daily life. He has not hesitated, therefore, to give, in accordance with the views of Mr. Wiley, the following examples and explanations. They refer to those points connected with the state of ventilation that have most forcibly arrested his attention in the United States, and are arranged in a form that will enable those not professionally acquainted with the subject, to trace their bearings on the condition of their own habitations.

Observations made at the Academy of Medicine by Dr. Francis and other members of the profession, an address by Dr. Stevens, printed in the State papers at Albany, and the very able works on Ventilation published in the United States by Dr. Wyman, Dr. Griscom, and Dr. Bell, as well as publications and papers by Dr. Jarvis of Dorchester, Dr. Stone of Washington, and Dr. Barton of New Orleans, have convinced the author that the importance of this subject is widely acknowledged and supported with great energy, ability, and zeal on this, as well as on the other side of the Atlantic, however imperfect the ideas and practice of the great masses of the population may still be in respect to it both in the old and the new world. On the subject of quarantine, that concentrates more ventilating questions than any other department of sanitary improvement, he was fortunate enough to be introduced, by the Board of Health of the City of New York, to Dr. Harris, whose practice with such resources as were within his power, was full of interest, while nothing could be more significant than the desertion of the principal building intended for hospital accommodation, in consequence of its imperfect and unsatisfactory ventilation. His important and elaborate report on yellow fever and other infectious diseases, presented to the Legislature during the last year, shows how attentively and practically the various phenomena and causes of such diseases have been studied by him, and points emphatically to the course that should be pursued on this great and interesting question.

The limits and nature of a volume intended more for the general than the professional reader, do not allow the opportunity of acknowledging all the varied, interesting, and valuable facts that have been brought under notice in the works published or in the inventions seen here. But it may at least be remarked, that whatever advantages may be claimed in Europe, in systematic ventilation, mild heating surfaces, and hot water apparatus, greater perfection has been attained here in some varieties of steam apparatus, blowers, and arrangements for the use of Anthracite coal, than are met with in other places. In reference to the latter, in some parts of England, and still more in many places in Wales and Ireland, were some of the many ingenious stoves introduced that are in daily use in this country, in small apartments, they would be a great improvement to some of the arrangements at present resorted to in the use of this coal, if combined with due ventilation.

Public works, now in progress, or lately completed, more especially at Washington, Boston, New York, and Philadelphia, equally attest the attention that is at present given to ventilation in the United States; and public proceedings at numerous medical associations, at the Smithsonian Institution at Washington, under the direction of Professor Henry, at the Lowell Institute at Boston, and at the Boards of Health in New York and other cities, show the interest taken in this subject. The works on education, and the Educational Journal of the Hon. Henry Barnard of Hartford, and the report of the Committee of the Academy of Medicine on the National Hotel disease, at Washington, afford some of the most recent proofs and expositions of the magnitude and importance of the practical questions it involves.

But no one can have examined the state of ventilation, either in the old or in the new world, without being satisfied that, whatever may have been done in particular places, good ventilation, combined with systematic arrangements both for heating and cooling, is the exception, and not the rule in all classes of buildings. The testimony of Dr. Griscom, of the Hon. Henry Barnard, and of the Inspector of Schools in Brooklyn, presents striking and important evidence on this point as to one class of buildings that demands the most scrupulous consideration, particularly where the capacity and energy of the lungs are apt to fall below the proper standard, in early youth, from the want of due facilities for daily exercise and appropriate play-ground.

To the city inspector in New York, and in other cities, as well as many official authorities, particularly in connexion with the Board of Emigration and quarantine establishments, special acknowledgments are due by the author for the opportunities afforded him in inquiries as to the condition of public health.

The essential element of all ventilation consisting in the ingress and egress of air, it appears to be an extremely simple subject to those who take no further thought of it. But modes and details of action require to be studied and multiplied, according to the peculiarities in the structure of different buildings, the wants and occupations of individual constitutions, and the number crowded on a given space. In some places a simple aperture satisfies every want, if there be sufficient skill and knowledge to use it judiciously. In others, the extremes of heat and cold, dryness and moisture, malaria and mosquitoes render precautions and resources desirable, that can be made to contribute largely to the security of health and to the improvement of comfort in all classes of dwellings.

But a great work is still to be done. The practice of ventilation requires to be brought home to the habitations of masses of the population, and their sympathies enlisted in its principles, and extended to all classes of buildings and sanitary improvements. An extended and united co-operation among all classes of society, and between the medical, the architectural, the engineering, and the agricultural professions, in forwarding the cause of public health, is still a desideratum. Without their combined efforts it is impossible for town and country to reciprocate all the mutual advantages they can confer on each other, and to develope a complete system of architecture, where beauty, utility, and economy shall each have their legitimate influence, while oppressive atmospheres and accidents by fire shall no longer be of such frequent occurrence in any class of buildings. It is confessed, however, that without the general introduction of instruction in the leading truths of practical science in connexion with the chemistry and physiology of daily life, in all schools and academies, and suitable experimental illustrations, there can be no great expectation that all classes will share, as they might do, in the fruits of the progress of discovery. Nor can the sanitary question subserve those great religious, moral, and economic results that would tend most materially to increase the duration of human life, and enable man to participate more largely in all the blessings and bounties which a beneficent and omnipotent Providence has placed within his stewardship and control during his transitory existence in this world, if the seed be not sown that shall give the key of the material world freely to the rising generation, and enable it to weave the principles and practice of science with the wants of humanity in the affairs of daily life.

CONTENTS.

———•◦•———

DIAGRAMS.

––––––►◄––––––

AN INTRODUCTORY OUTLINE

OF THE

PROGRESS OF SANITARY IMPROVEMENT.

THE Homes of the people, or the conditions of domiciliary life, furnish most reliable indices of the state of intellectual and moral advancement in any community. Though it cannot be assumed that the improvement of man's physical condition will alone secure his moral elevation, it is unquestionably true that it contributes essentially to that important end, and that neither intellectual progress nor moral and social refinement can be long maintained where the requisite conditions for physical health and comfort are not suitably provided.

Our bodily senses, or the faculties by which we are enabled to appreciate the real qualities of the material world, were manifestly given by our beneficent Creator for the purpose of guiding to that which is desirable and good, and for our protection from all that is physically disagreeable, and injurious. Poisonous gases, noxious emanations, and the oppressive sensations produced by stagnant air and mephitic odors give timely warning of the danger, disease, and death, that are incurred by continued exposure to such unwholesome agencies. And while the olfactory sense is thus ever active and indispensably serviceable in guarding against evils unseen, the eye is continually revealing to the mind all those relations of forms and colors, which by their beauty and fitness afford satisfaction, or by deformity and unfitness produce dissatisfaction or disgust. So the ear, which ministers to the human soul some of its richest pleasures, may also transmit irritating sounds and produce distracting sensations; and by a wonderful development and provision of the nervous system, the human body is enabled to *feel* its relations to the material world,—experiencing comfort and delight, or irritation and pain.

That the means for promoting personal comfort and physical health are within the reach, and measurably under the control of man, is no less true than that the love of happiness and the principle of self-preservation are instinctive in the human race.

It is too true that ignorance, poverty, want, and disease, exclude from large classes the means of enjoying some of the most important requisites for their temporal welfare; but it is also true, that in accordance with the great laws of unity in human interests, whatever improvements may be necessary to secure the general health and welfare of the ignorant and the poor, constitute, at the same time, truly essential conditions for the protection and well-being of the more favored classes. Especially is this unity of interests made manifest in the hygienic conditions of populous towns and cities. The close, uncleansed, unventilated residences of the poor become the homes of disease and pauperism; the crowded narrow tenements to which avarice drives poverty, in filthy streets and noisome courts, become perennial sources of deadly miasmata that may be wafted to the neighboring mansions of wealth and refinement, to cause sickness and mourning there; and when once the breath of pestilence becomes epidemic in any city, commerce and trade are driven to more salubrious marts.

The promotion of personal and public hygiene, and a proper provision for the physical necessities and moral interests of our fellow men, seem, therefore, to be alike demanded by the soundest principles of political economy and the precepts of Christian duty.

We hail with pleasure such a work as this of Dr. Reid's, which is designed to reach the homes and the wants of all classes of our population; in a plain and practical manner, giving instruction in regard to that most essential requisite for universal health and comfort,—a pure atmosphere in every human habitation;—a theme that occupied the mind of Howard in his visits to the abodes of disease and woe, and one which made the name of Count Rumford known in every hamlet and workshop in Europe, though the grand desideratum was not attained in the days of those great men, nor yet, except as regards temperature, even by the ingenuity of our own Dr. Franklin and Dr. Nott.

Having been requested by the publishers of this treatise, to furnish an outline of the progress of improvement in ventilation, and also a sketch of the public labors of Dr. Reid, we propose briefly to notice some of the more important steps of such progress, and to present those principles and facts relating to this department of hygienic improvement which need to be more generally understood and appreciated.

In pastoral life, and among the more barbarous tribes of our race, man has usually enjoyed the invigorating influences of the natural atmosphere during his wakeful hours; but from the earliest history of architectural structures and of civilization, in his attempts to provide against the inclemency of the elements, and to secure the means of domestic comfort and luxury, he has too often shut out from his habitation the fresh air of heaven, and confined a deleterious atmosphere within the choicest apartments of his dwelling. The styles of building adopted by the earlier nations of antiquity, as far as they are at present known to us, made very imperfect provisions for warming, light, or ventilation. The Phœnicians, the Egyptians, and after them the Hebrews in Palestine, the Babylonians, and the Greeks, made great improvements in architecture and the provisions for domestic comfort; yet the dwellings of those people were very imperfectly supplied with a comfortable and healthy atmosphere during the more inclement period of the year. Artificial warmth was imparted to the air of the apartments solely by open fires without a chimney, and the offensive, stagnant atmosphere of unventilated apartments was deodorized by pungent or agreeable perfumes; yet it is true, that upon the roofs and in the open courts of ancient oriental dwellings, a pure atmosphere could be enjoyed.

Though the Greeks and Romans, in their highest state of civilization and refinement, developed styles of general architecture which must forever excite the admiration of the world, yet neither in their public nor their private edifices, were there such provisions and appliances for controlling the temperature and securing ventilation as to provide an agreeable atmosphere during the cold season.

That the importance of thorough ventilation was appreciated, how-ever, in its relation to the preservation of health, would seem evident from several sources. We are informed, for example, by Varro, that several cities in Greece were preserved by Hippocrates from an epidemic pestilence, by a proper adjustment of the windows or aper-tures of the dwellings in those cities, thus securing a constant through-draft. Celsus, also, recommends a large room for a person ill of fever; or a small fire to be made in it to clear the air. But it would appear that the great deficiency in the structure of all habitations in ancient days consisted, as in more modern times, in a lack of suitable means for warming the air without vitiating it. To avoid this difficulty, we find the younger Pliny so arranging and constructing his delightful Laurentine villa, as to secure the greatest possible advantages from that natural source of heat, the sun, added to most ingenious archi-tectural devices for protection from wintry winds. Similar architec-tural arrangements have been observed, in some instances, in the struc-ture of the disentombed palaces of Pompeii.

A simple but cumbersome apparatus for heating, known as the hypocaust, was in common use for warming apartments and baths among the Romans; and though it must have been very expensive on account of the great amount of fuel required, it appears to have answered many desirable purposes, and was esteemed a source of great luxury in the cold season. This contrivance for artificial warming was introduced by the Romans into the various northern countries conquered by them; but it never came into general use except among the wealthy classes. In its most highly perfected form, the hypocaust might have been used as an aid to the ventilation of apartments, as in its structure it somewhat resembled a modern house furnace, having pipes or flues communicating from the great oven or fire-chamber, to the several apartments above, the tubes or flues being closed until the fire had ceased to glow, and then opened at pleasure, like a hot-air register in a modern house. In several costly villas, erected by the Roman conquerors in Great Britain, traces of the hypocaust have been found. In the remains of a villa at Woodchester, supposed to have been erected by order of the Emperor Adrian, and containing sixty-five apartments, the works for warming were carried to a high degree of perfection, all the main passages and apartments being supplied with hypocausts, or hot-air flues therefrom.

But, whatever may have been the condition of the atmosphere in the more costly residences of early times, in various countries, it is known that the common people in Great Britain dwelt in structures of the rudest kind, and spent most of their time, and sought all their sports, in the open air. Human habitations were almost universally close, dingy, and damp; and until the chimney and its fire-place came into use, in the fourteenth and fifteenth centuries, all dwellings were rendered unendurable by smoke and its deleterious constituents.

It is said that the use of chimneys originated in Italy, in the early part of the fourteenth century; and they were common in Venice at a little later period. This important appendage to the human dwelling, constituting as it does a grand ventilating shaft, as well as a flue for the escape of smoke and offensive gases, has long been an indispensable source of comfort and health to mankind; and until plans for systematic ventilation can be applied in every modern dwelling, we are bound to protest against the practice, now so common, of closing those flues, which so cheaply, though, it may be, very imperfectly, perform the function of natural ventilators.

During the sixteenth century, the population of large towns in Great Britain suffered much from fatal fevers, known as the sweating sickness, the pestilence, etc. Populous districts were decimated from time to time, and the people justly regarded these deadly maladies with great horror. It was during that interesting period of British history, also, that the memorable pestilence of jail fever, repeatedly and suddenly broke forth, at the opening of the overcrowded and unventilated prisons at the assizes. At the time of the celebrated Black Assize at Oxford, in the year 1577, it is stated that six hundred persons sickened in a single night, and that five hundred and ten persons died of the fever in the course of a few days. The fatal outbursts of fever that have occurred at the Old Bailey, in London, in later years, were of similar character, and their history is better known to us. Those terrible visitations, as well as most of the great epidemics of fever, which repeatedly desolated the rapidly-growing cities of England, appear to have arisen from the gross neglect of domiciliary and public hygiene. In a Royal Proclamation issued in 1602, it is stated by the Queen, "that heretofore, in her princelie wisdom and providence, she had foreseen the great and manifold inconveniences and mischiefs which did then grow by the accesse and confluence of the people; and that such great multitudes being brought to inhabit in such small rooms, whereof a great part being very poor, and being heaped up together, and in a sort smothered with many families of children and servants in one house, or small tenement, it must needs follow that if ane plague, or other universal sickness should, by God's permission, enter among these multitudes, the same would spread itself, out of which neither her Majestie's own person, but by God's special providence, nor any other whatsoever, could be exempted."

"This prophetic warning," says an eloquent writer, "was fearfully realized about seven months afterwards, when the plague swept off thirty-seven thousand citizens between April and November."

What was true of London and other cities of England, was equally true respecting the causes and prevalence of disease in all European cities,—habitual neglect of public cleanliness, neglect of proper drainage and sewerage, and inattention to domestic ventilation and purity, were continual sources of pestilential maladies, which more than equalled war and religious persecution in the desolations they caused.

The great plague that prevailed in London during the year 1665, and the sanitary effects of the great fire, which took place in 1666, sweeping over the densely-built streets and unventilated quarters, where the pestilence had originated, did much to awaken public attention to the domestic causes of disease. In the brief period of about four months, upwards of one hundred thousand persons perished in London from the plague. Four thousand were known to have expired in a single night, and during the months of July and August fifty thousand dead bodies were cast from the dead carts into the common pits; the victims being chiefly of the lowest sort of people, who lived in circumstances of great filth and foul air.

An historian of that period states, that during the prevalence of this pestilence, there was an uninterrupted *calm*, so that there was not air sufficient to turn a vane; and a distinguished modern writer, in giving an account of the terrible visitation, remarks that "the *want of ventilation in the houses* concurred with the moist, warm, calm air out of doors, or, in other words, with the want of wind, the great ventilator of nature, every squalid inmate of an ill-ventilated apartment became a reeking sphere of pestilence, impregnating the motionless air of his dwelling and neighborhood with the fatal elements of a loathsome death." He adds, also "One cannot contemplate without astonishment, the delusive and futile means that were followed to arrest and mitigate the dire contagion; nor think without humiliation, that *opinions* prevented reliance on the promptings of nature, to keep themselves clean, or to admit fresh air into their habitations, the only rational and effectual means of escape from danger; and by following which, modern physicians not only prevent infection and make it harmless, but have eradicated the epidemical plague itself from England."

The city which rose phœnix-like from the ashes of the fire, was indeed a new town, and the regenerating influences of that unparallelled conflagration continue to the present day. The immediate effects of the rebuilding and improvements were most marked. An historian of that day, says " the inhabitants moved in a large sphere of *pure air*, and seeing and feeling everything sweet and new around them, they perhaps wished to keep them so. A man of moderate fortune saw his house superior in its fittings and comforts, to the palatial rooms built in the time of his grandfather. When he paced the streets, he felt the genial western breeze pass him rich with the perfume of the country, and looking upward he beheld the beautiful azure sky variegated with fleecy clouds in place of projecting beams, black windows, stories, and spouts, obscured and blackened with smoke and dirt."

Great improvements were made in domestic architecture during the latter part of the seventeenth century, not only in Great Britain, but throughout Europe. The houses were better ventilated by improved arrangements of their various passages, apartments, and openings. More abundant provision was made for the admission of *light*, that indispensable requisite for health; window sashes were made to be movable, so as to secure at pleasure greater supplies of fresh air; and as early as the beginning of the last century, we find ingenious men calling attention to the importance of more perfect ventilation in public buildings. Sir Christopher Wren, the renowned architect, gave his attention to this important subject, and endeavored, though unsuccessfully, to provide suitable ventilation for the Houses of Parliament. In 1723, an ingenious Frenchman, named Desaguliers, was called upon to remedy the defective atmosphere of those houses, and he is said to have succeeded in a tolerable degree—without disturbing the architecture as left by Sir Christopher; the improvement adopted at that period in the House of Commons was essentially upon the principle of *thermo-ventilation*, or ventilation by heated air shafts; and some years afterwards, the same gentleman proposed to introduce into private dwellings, hospitals, and prisons, appliances for renovating the atmosphere without opening the doors or windows. This he designed to accomplish mainly by the use of a *fanner* or blowing-wheel.

Dr. Hales, soon after this time, devoted himself with remarkable enthusiasm and intelligence to the work of improving the ventilation of all classes of buildings, and he made many ingenious experiments and original investigations relating to the physical properties of the atmospheric air, which, together with the great discoveries in its chemistry, gave a decided impulse to efforts for sanitary improvement.

The occurrence of a terribly fatal pestilence at the opening of the Spring Assizes at the Old Bailey, in London, in 1750, startled the public mind, as did, also, many sad disasters which about that period befell large companies of British troops in overcrowded vessels at sea, and in unventilated barracks on land. The horrors of the middle passage in the slave trade had also become widely known, and its causes of mortality understood. In his benevolent efforts to alleviate the untold sufferings that filled the prisons and lazarettos at that day, the philanthropic Howard made praiseworthy attempts to improve the unhealthy atmosphere of such establishments by causing openings to be made near the ceiling of each department, and by hanging the window sashes on pivots so as to secure, when open, a current of fresh air with a slanting direction upwards towards the ceiling. But his noble efforts, and his

methods for improving the condition of the ventilation proved very
uncertain and unsatisfactory. That great philanthropist made very
important practical suggestions, however, respecting plans for a more
complete system of ventilation in all new prisons and asylums. As
another good result of Howard's suggestions respecting the causes of
disease in prisons, we find an act in 1775 empowering magistrates to
order the ceilings and walls of such buildings to be "scraped and white-
washed once a year at least, and supplied with fresh air by hand-venti-
lators or otherwise."

During the year previous to the ingenious invention made by Dr.
FRANKLIN for improvement in the mode of warming apartments, in
1784, St. Thomas' Hospital, in London, was greatly improved in its
ventilation, by cutting away a small portion from the lower panes in
the upper sash of each window. The result to the patients was highly
beneficial.

With the labors of Desaguliers, Sutton, Hales, and Howard, valuable improvements were introduced, and a host of inventors and scientific men contributed to the good work already so well begun. Count
Rumford devoted his energies to improvements in warming, and the
perfection of the chimney; and so satisfactory and extensively useful
were his labors, that the people justly recognised him as a great bene-
factor, and whole cities were ready to do him homage. And our own
Franklin shared with him the enviable distinction of *patron of fireside
comfort.*

In the United States, we have adopted, in rapid succession, all the
improvements that have been made in Great Britain and Europe, and in
many departments of domestic economy and hygiene, our people have
made great advances. The styles of our architecture, both in our cities
and our rural districts, bear the impress of American progress. Most
of our cities and large towns are furnished with an ample supply of
pure water, an element almost as indispensable to personal health and
happiness, as sunlight and the air we breathe. The claims of the poor
and the ignorant upon wealth, knowledge, and power, are perhaps
more attentively and justly regarded here than in any other country;
and neither health, life, property, nor civil institutions can long be

secure among any people, where such claims and necessities of the lower classes of society are not scrupulously regarded.

But our cities and towns, and all our rural homes, have great hygienic wants, which loudly demand the attention of the physician, the philanthropist, and the public-spirited citizen. In most of our large towns and cities, a general disregard of suitable architectural provisions for a proper supply of sunlight and fresh air, with great inattention to cleanliness and drainage, are continually acting causes of disease and general deterioration of the public health ; while, in the dwellings of our rural population, we too often find, even where great general intelligence prevails, that the most essential conditions of domestic health and comfort are sadly lost sight of, in the attempt to amass wealth, or to practise an economy of means and space that does not contemplate the requirements of the laws of life and health, nor provide in a proper manner for a suitable supply of fresh air, pure water, and good external ventilation. Too frequently, even in the most pleasant country districts, are building sites selected without a proper reference to those external hygienic conditions which are most essential to the continued enjoyment of health.

In malarious districts, and wherever there exists any local nuisance, or any natural or artificial obstruction to complete natural ventilation from the prevailing or the dryest winds, it is of primary importance that the location of the site for a dwelling be carefully selected with reference to all these hygienic considerations. We are happy to see that Dr. Reid has devoted a chapter especially to this subject. (See Chap. xxxii.) A timely suggestion on these topics, or in regard to domestic cleanliness, disinfection, ventilation, or drainage, might have saved many interesting families we have known, from painful sicknesses and untimely mourning.

The sanitary condition and hygienic protection of large cities have engaged the attention of physicians and statesmen from the earliest ages of civic life; it is but recently, however, that much anxiety or interest has been felt on this subject in our American cities.

Our great marts of commerce have at length become so densely populated, and so compactly built; while relatively, as well as numerically, there has been a vast increase in the proportion of poverty and ignorance among the masses of the people in our midst, arriving as most of them have from foreign lands, that the plainest principles of self-protection, as well as the conservation of the public health and morals, demand a scrutinizing investigation not only of the sanitary conditions of domiciliary life in these crowded cities, but likewise a strict municipal and scientific surveillance of all removable causes of disease, whether in tenement houses or hotels, in private squares or public institutions, or in the drainage and sewerage, the supply of water, and the provisions for universal cleanliness and disinfection.

The sanitary condition of the city of New York may be taken as a fair example of the hygienic wants of most of our large towns; and we need only refer to a few facts to illustrate the imperative necessity of giving prompt and efficient attention to the removable sources of danger and disease which exist in our communities.

First, We would refer to the fact that more than one-half the entire population of the city of New York reside in crowded tenement houses, and that there is no statute or municipal law regulating the construction, ventilation, or the space allowed to specified numbers of residents therein. Hence crowding such structures to their utmost capacity has become the rule rather than the exception. And it may here be stated, that our city has an underground or cellar population of more than twenty-five thousand persons.

In the 17th ward alone, there are 1,257 tenement houses, having 20,917 rooms, which are occupied by 10,128 families, embracing a total number of 51,172 persons; thus giving an average of about four persons to each suite of two apartments, one only of which is usually occupied as a dormitory, and that one often a dark close room, of a capacity only of from 500 to 800 cubic feet. Now, in a close apartment of only 600 cubic feet, a single person cannot spend six consecutive hours, in air of ordinary temperature, without impairment of health.

Dr. Reid's estimate of ten cubic feet of pure air per minute, for the respiration of an- adult person, is certainly quite low enough for an average of comfort and safety, and with such an allowance, the air in such an apartment would become too much vitiated for healthy respiration at the expiration of sixty minutes or one hour; and allowing that the air is partially replenished during that brief period, the atmosphere would be decidedly unwholesome at the expiration of two or three hours. Or, taking the lowest estimate within the limits of safety, as given by Dr. Neill Arnott, viz., about three cubic feet per minute, such an apartment could not be considered a healthy sleeping-room for a single person, much less, a safe dormitory for a whole family.

In some of the lower wards of the city the tenement houses are much more densely crowded than in those just mentioned. In one of them, containing from 120 to 150 families of three to ten persons each, there are but about forty feet of frontage and sunlight. In two of the smallest of those apartments eight cases of malignant typhus have been seen at one time. And at the last visitation of cholera, the first cases of that malady occurred in that pent up and overcrowded locality.

Second, Small-pox, typhus fever, and every other pestilence, find a genial and prolific soil in such crowded unventilated structures as the habitations of the poor in our city, and from them the germs of fatal diseases are continually conveyed to the dwellings of the more favored classes.

Third, The fashionable and gregarious custom of crowding our hotels and boarding-houses is becoming a hazardous practice, unless more attention is given to the hygienic condition and wants of such establishments—very few of which have hitherto been provided with anything like systematic and efficient ventilation, or perfect drainage. The recent fearful endemic at the National Hotel, in the city of Washington, should teach an important practical lesson on this subject.

Fourth, The drainage or sewerage, and the necessary measures for securing general cleanliness and a pure atmosphere, are not yet suitably provided for by law.

Fifth, Architecture, in its application to private residences as well as to public edifices, has not yet had primary or suitable reference to man's hygienic interests. Adaptations for a sufficient supply of pure air and sunlight have been sacrificed to architectural effect on the one hand, and to a mistaken economy on the other.

The vital importance of a correct understanding and estimation of such considerations as the foregoing, must be manifest to all who intelligently investigate such subjects; and to the political economist, the merchant, and the moralist, these topics are invested with relations quite as interesting as those that lead the physician and the philanthropist to study them.

Frequently have eminent statesmen been forced to investigate the causes of diseases and consequent commercial decay in cities. The great plague at Athens, which occurred in the time of Pericles, was so obviously the result of overcrowding and civic uncleanliness, that the Athenians were enraged against him for having caused the deadly distemper, by inviting the people of Attica, during the Peloponnesian war, to flock in vast multitudes into Athens, until the city became excessively crowded. Plutarch informs us that the enemies of Pericles boldly attempted to ruin him by reiterating the fact, which was, alas, too true, that the sanitary interests of the city had not been properly regarded by its Great Archon.

In Great Britain, from the days of Henry the VIII. and Queen Elizabeth, to the present time, the sanitary question has excited the interest, and enlisted the services of the ablest men. The most important effort ever undertaken in any country for general sanitary improvement and reform, was the "Health of Towns Commission," which was organized by the reigning Queen in the year 1843, under the title of "*The Commission for Inquiring into the State of Large Towns and Populous Districts.*"

This Board of Commissioners was composed of thirteen distinguished scientific and philanthropic gentlemen, among whom was the Duke of Buccleugh, the Earl of Lincoln, Sir Thomas de la Beche, Dr. David Boswell Reid, Dr. Lyon Playfair, and Richard Owen. The stupendous results of their investigations and labors may be judged of by their final Reports, which are comprised in three huge folios, every page of which is full of most instructive facts. Probably no other attempt at Sanitary reform has produced results at all comparable with this.

We would here quote the following suggestive remarks from the concluding paragraphs of that remarkable Report, as very correctly illustrating the relations of the Sanitary question in our own country, as well as in Great Britain. After stating their views and giving their advice upon all the various questions assigned for their investigation, the Commissioners in closing the Report to their Sovereign, say,—

"In submitting to your Majesty the measures we recommend for ameliorating the physical condition of the population, inhabiting large towns and populous districts, by improvements in drainage, cleansing, ventilation, and the supply of water, we must again express our deep conviction of the extent, importance, and difficulty of the subject—a conviction strengthened by the continuance of our investigations. The most important evils affecting the public health throughout England and Wales, are characterized by little variety, *and it is only in the degree of their intensity, that the towns exhibit the worst examples of such evils.* Villages and clusters of houses inhabited by the poor, are often under the influence of the same causes of disease, though their effect in such situations may be rendered comparatively slight *from the more free circulation of the external air.* The vitiation of the atmosphere from over-crowding, and the absence of proper ventilation in individual apartments, produces in the rural districts the same diseases that arise from the same causes in a town population."

Under our republican form of government, it may not be practicable to carry out all great sanitary reforms by the aid of special legislation, yet it is evident that our state and municipal authorities can do much to urge forward any measures that may be required for the preservation of the public health; and still more certainly, would all the great objects of improvement in personal and public hygiene be attained, by means of the universal diffusion of knowledge on the subjects of chemistry, human physiology, and the laws of life.

Those who understand and appreciate the relations which these departments of knowledge sustain to human welfare, and the improvement of society, should heartily engage in efforts for its general diffusion among the people; and to this end, the most persevering personal efforts are requisite. In our primary schools, our academies, and universities, greater attention should be given to these highly practical and universally important departments of learning; books, periodicals, and illustrated works on these subjects, adapted to the common wants of all classes, should be found in every library and every household in the land; and special lectures with practical demonstrations on these interesting topics, should occasionally be given in all our villages and school districts.

Architecture must be studied and practised as an art upon which the principles of vital chemistry, and human physiology, have claims, no less important than the laws of mechanics, and the strength of materials, and in which the laws of health and the claims of personal comfort should ever be paramount to architectural embellishment and artistic effect.

The architect should be as thoroughly educated for his important profession, as the physician or the jurist is instructed for his.

Several of our American citizens have made most praiseworthy efforts to awaken public attention to the vast importance of proper ventilation, and an improved architecture for American dwellings and public edifices. A few persons have also written and labored with intelligence and earnestness on topics connected with the practical applications of chemistry and physiology to the concerns and interests of daily life. Among these gentlemen, may be mentioned the names of Dr. John H. Griscom, Mr. Edward L. Youmans, Mr. Wyman and Hon. Henry Barnard; while among recent writers in Europe, as well as in our own country, stands more prominently perhaps than any other, the name of Dr. D. B. Reid.

Without any discredit to others, it may justly be said that in systematic efforts for the improvement of domestic as well as public architecture, with reference to the demands of the laws of life and health; in the varied applications of chemistry to the wants of daily life, and in plans and works for the general diffusion of knowledge on these subjects, Dr. Reid has not only been a pioneer, but he remains a most practical and untiring advocate. The relations which he has held, and still continues to sustain, to the most important plans and works for sanitary reform, and hygienic and educational improvements, will justify, in this place, a brief sketch of some of his more important labors connected with improvements in ventilation.

The actual state of all the practically important questions and principles relating to ventilation, and a proper supply of air in all classes of buildings, previous to Dr. Reid's investigations and public labors, may be correctly estimated from the testimony that was given before a Select Committee of the British Parliament in the year 1835. We quote the following from the evidence of Dr. Birkbeck, a scientific gentleman who had given much attention to the subject of venti-lation :—

"I have never seen a room ventilated, with strict reference to the whole purposes of ventilation; where it has been done at all systema-tically, it has consisted in making a certain number of openings in the lower part of the room, and a certain number of openings in the upper part of the room, often without any correspondence to their areas, and often without any supply of air to the lower openings, or any suitable means of escape for the air from the upper." Speaking of the venti-lation of the Houses of Parliament at that period, he says emphatically, "The smothering system adopted at present is terrible; I am sure, I for one, would not endure it for the service of the public."

Similar statements may truthfully be made respecting most of the public buildings, churches, and private residences, in the United States at the present day; proper arrangements for a suitable supply of pure fresh air being rarely provided for in architectural designs.

We hail with pleasure, therefore, the distinguished Author of the fol-lowing chapters, who is widely known as an enlightened and enthusiastic pioneer and laborer, in plans and works for the improvement of the physical and moral condition of the people. For more than a quarter of a century, in addition to important public services, he has, in pro-moting improved ventilation, been an earnest advocate and projector of measures for the more universal diffusion of scientific knowledge, and its application to the arts and affairs of daily life.

Preceded in this class of philosophic efforts by such men as Count Rumford, Dr. Franklin, Tredgold, and Sir Humphry Davy, Dr. Reid's labors have not been less important nor less practical than were the works of those great friends of humanity and science. Indeed, in *his special department*, he has, perhaps, more fully than any other man, entered into and carried forward the spirit of their labors, in the application of science to the wants of common life.

Though Dr. Reid's name has become especially associated with the progress of ventilation, as applied to public buildings, a great portion of his life has been devoted to works for the general improvement of society. In attempting to sketch the progress of ideas relating to domiciliary improvement, and the ventilation of dwellings and public buildings, we are compelled to refer to certain leading events in the history of Dr. Reid's personal labors and public services.

Thoroughly educated as a physician, and in his early professional services in the Medical Charities of his native city, made familiar with the great causes of disease, and with the hygienic wants of domestic life, Dr. Reid very naturally turned his attention to the study of those physical causes and conditions, which are most widely extended and active in the production of ill health among the people. His position as a lecturer on Chemistry afforded opportunities for arousing public attention to the *removable causes of disease ;* and he faithfully labored to enlighten the public mind on this subject.

Though the chemical properties of atmospheric air and the gases had been carefully investigated and learnedly discussed by Lavoisier, Scheele, Priestley, Black, and their successors; and although from Hippocrates to Hales and Beddoes, the causative and the curative relations of air to disease had been observed; while Davy, Menzies, Dalton, Edwards, Graham, and a crowd of experimenters had fully investigated the Chemistry of the atmosphere and of respiration, and had studied the laws governing the diffusion of gases, it remained for Dr. Reid to determine by practical experiments made on living men, by means of apparatus, and in rooms constructed specially for this purpose, the precise amount of air required for health and comfort; the circumstances under which it can be supplied effectually in accordance with the ever-varying demands of the human frame; and with due allowance for all the peculiarities of climates, constitutions, and the different classes of habitations, ships, and buildings. In addition to his varied experiments and analyses in his laboratory, he devised great practical illustrations of the true principles of ventilation, combining at once simplicity, economy, and efficiency.

In 1833, Dr. Reid completed a new lecture-room and also a practical

class-room, both of which were appropriated entirely to experimental purposes. They were provided with special means for warming, lighting, and
ventilation, and also with peculiar flues for directly removing the vitiated
gases and vapors evolved in the experiments made either by himself or
his pupils. The ground enclosed at first was eighty feet square, to which
additions were afterwards made, and on which five rooms were built,
that were devoted to investigations and illustrations of his views in
reference to sanitary and architectural objects.* The experiments
made in this building laid the foundation of plans that were afterwards
executed by Dr. Reid.

The following is a brief outline of the leading points that were advocated in the introduction of his system of ventilation.

1. A much larger allowance of air than that which had been previously given in estimates; and the foundation of all such estimates in
unison with the number of persons to be supplied in a given time, and
not on the cubic contents of the apartments to be ventilated.

2. The introduction of means for applying power at all times when

* The following is a brief description of the building. The principal part of the
roof was supported by fourteen pillars, which, being arranged in two rows, formed a
great central colonnade. Each of those pillars being hollow, constituted a fire and
ventilating flue that could command four or more furnaces at its base; while the
upper portion of each was perforated with a series of apertures provided with valves
which afforded a ventilating power at any required level.

Below the floor, flues traversed the ground in every direction; the action of
many of which could be combined, whenever increased local ventilation was
desired. Larger shafts or chimneys with a cupola, a steam engine, a forge, with
metallurgic furnaces, and ventilated sand baths, were added to all the peculiar
apparatus used in chemical experiments, and to the experimental tables provided for
students.

The Lecture table was forty feet long: it was furnished with furnaces at the
centre, and in the wall at each end. Steam, gas, a red heat, and ventilating power
with descending currents, could be secured whenever they were wanted. Behind
the Lecturer, on a more elevated platform, another range of furnaces and apparatus,
forty feet in length, was also provided, which illustrated all the principal operations
in the chemical arts, and gave great power and resources in chemical investigations.
These works contributed materially to the greatly increased attention that was soon
afterwards paid to ventilation and sanitary improvement.

requisite for the ventilation of buildings, and the sustaining of a *plenum* vacuum*, or an equalized movement of air, according to the perfection required in the ventilating arrangements.

3. The more extended arrangements by valves, or other means for varying with facility, the supply of air given in different conditions of the atmosphere at assemblies, subject to long sittings, and to great and sudden fluctuations in the number attending.

4. The importance in all public buildings, of providing channels for the supply and discharge of air, entirely separate and apart from doors and windows; and the introduction of double glazing, or other means to prevent the cooling or heating influence of ordinary windows, when subjected to extreme heat or cold.

5. The more uniform supply of fresh air by diffusion, regulated with regard to quantity, by the number of persons present, and the magnitude of the building.

6. The formation of extended arrangements for supplying air from the purest accessible source; for excluding or covering local impurities; for cooling, drying, and moistening air; and for the entire and absolute isolation of the warming and ventilating power, so as to permit the latter to be used in full force in warm weather.

7. The introduction of exclusive lighting, or ventilated lamps, wherever the currents do not certainly remove the products of combustion from the lights in use.

8. The determination of ascending, descending, or compound movements of air, and of the circumstances which should regulate their adoption.

---

* A Plenum movement, or *plenum ventilation*, is that in which there is an *excess of air within*, and an escape accordingly from doors or crevices, *the air blowing outwards*. In *Vacuum ventilation*, on the other hand, leakage at doors and crevices moves inwards; the air within not being able to resist the pressure from without. In the third variety, which may be termed, *The equalized method of ventilation, the pressure caused by the entering of fresh air from without is made to equalize as far as possible the draught of the escaping vitiated air*, so that there is little or no tendency to draughts of air at doors and crevices. The air moves in and out, solely by its appropriate channels.

9. The formation of ventilated rooms or chambers for artificial atmospheres, and their application in the cure of diseases.

10. The development of a more uniform and homogeneous architecture, in which acoustics, lighting, warming, cooling, ventilating, and fire-proofing, should enter more largely into the original design, and be made a primary instead of a secondary object in determining the various details, &c., of the construction.

11. The improvement of external ventilation, and of effective sanitary measures necessary to secure that object.

12. The decomposition, absorption, or condensation of noxious gases from manufactories or from other sources.

The means of accomplishing the various objects enumerated, have been so fully attained by Dr. Reid, in the varied combinations he has introduced, that but little remains to be desired, so far as relates to principles and practice; though the details present an inexhaustible field of improvement in the means, materials, and artistic arrangements best suited to different designs or modes of construction. The great desideratum, viz. power or force to control at pleasure the quality and greatly increased supply and displacement of air, as well as its introduction by large channels and corresponding valves, its diffusion, gentle equalization, humidity, purity, and temperature, have been so largely extended and so fully systematized by him, that we may properly consider them as constituting the prominent characteristics of his system of ventilation.

These improvements are justly regarded as the most important in the progress of ventilation, and their Author has given much time and labor to make them available in hospitals, ships, public buildings, private dwellings, coaches, mines, workshops, and every class of human habitations. In proportion as the public mind becomes enlightened on the subject, will these essential means of health and comfort be sought and enjoyed. The foregoing principles, which Dr. Reid so successfully attempted to illustrate in his own establishment at Edinburgh, were daily discussed and explained before his pupils, many of whom have since done good service in the great work of sanitary reform.

Few men have labored as assiduously to present to the people, the great practical conclusions and applications of science to the affairs of daily life. All Dr. Reid's efforts in public instruction, as well as his publications, have been pre-eminently practical and replete with common sense. Without enumerating them, we need only refer to his voluminous publications in his favorite department, Chemistry—one of which, issued by Messrs. Baillière, is significantly entitled the "Chemistry of Daily Life."

Dr. Reid's experiments and observations to ascertain the amount and proportions of fresh atmospheric air required for personal comfort and the preservation of health, were not confined to Great Britain; they were also conducted in numerous investigations in many of the cities of continental Europe; particularly Paris, Berlin, Munich, Stockholm, and St. Petersburg. They were extended to the air of crowded assemblies in churches, school-rooms, and workshops; and aided by his pupils at Edinburgh, he obtained specimens of vitiated air from such places, and subjected them to careful chemical analyses.

On the 16th of October, 1834, a destructive conflagration occurred at the Houses of Parliament, in London; and as new accommodations for the sessions of the British Legislature were thereby rendered necessary, many public men and members of Parliament felt great interest in improving the temporary halls of legislation, and in securing for the new houses a more perfect system of ventilation, warming, and acoustics, than had been enjoyed in the old Houses of Parliament.

During the month preceding the conflagration at the old Parliament Houses, the British Association had been convened at Edinburgh, in which city Dr. Reid had, for many years, been a distinguished and a successful instructor in chemistry and its applications. His vast laboratory and class-rooms were thronged with pupils from every quarter of the kingdom, and from various foreign nations; and those halls, erected from his designs and by his own direction, were themselves regarded as objects of great curiosity and interest,—practically illustrating the laws of ventilation and acoustics.

Members of the Association, and many Members of Parliament, having personally inspected this great practical school, which had been established by Dr. Reid, his ingenuity and scientific skill were at once sought in improving the temporary House of Commons, as a means of immediate relief there, and as the best mode of obtaining accurate information that might serve as a guide in the construction of the new buildings. The works in the former were speedily completed at a comparatively small expense, and they continued in use until the new houses were made ready for occupation—a period of some fifteen years—affording a remarkable degree of comfort and satisfaction to the members.

These plans, executed in three months, constituted the first systematic and thoroughly efficient works for ventilation ever carried out in any public building.

More than a century previously, somewhat similar labors had been undertaken at the old Houses of Parliament by Desaguliers, in improvement upon the works of Sir Christopher Wren; and still later, similar labors were undertaken by Sir Humphrey Davy, whose apparatus and provisions for ventilation, like those of his predecessors, had the great fault of *insufficiency and lack of power* for efficient and uniform ventilation.

Up to that period, the great object sought by the scientific directors of works for improvement in the ventilation and warming of those legislative halls, as well as of all other public buildings, seemed to have been too exclusively confined to measures for effectually *warming* the apartments,—the provisions for the escape of the vitiated atmosphere, and for the introduction of fresh air, being exceedingly meagre and unsatisfactory. As an example, we may refer to the old House of Peers, in which Sir Humphrey Davy used, for the discharge of the vitiated air of that hall, one or two tubes having a sectional area of *only one foot.* But in reconstructing the same hall for the temporary use of the House of Commons, Dr. Reid provided an aggregate area of *fifty feet* for the discharge of vitiated air. He had, in addition, a powerful shaft to determine any amount of movement, that a crowded attendance and the most sultry and oppressive atmosphere could require.

As might have been anticipated, the headaches, lethargy, somnolence, loss of appetite, and frequent ill health, so much complained of in the old house, with its indifferent and unequal ventilation, were never expe-

rienced in the reconstructed edifice when provided with an abundant supply of fresh air under the control of Dr. Reid's ingenious apparatus.*

* We have alluded to the condition of the ventilation in the old Houses of Parliament, previously to the introduction of Dr. Reid's plans. We are fully aware of
the severe criticisms and sweeping denunciations those plans called forth from certain parties; and it is not difficult to understand the origin and the animus of such
denunciations. Without referring to the personal and party interests and feel-
ings involved, we need only mention the fact, that the peculiar importance and real
blessings of pure fresh air are as often unappreciated by the great and the learned,
as by the poor and the ignorant, and like the blessings of temperance and virtue,
they are too often scorned.

But that Dr. Reid's improvements in the ventilation of the temporary House of
Commons were eminently successful, and to gentlemen capable of judging and
appreciating such improvements, perfectly satisfactory, we have incontrovertible
proofs. In justice to the principles involved in such questions, we cannot forbear
some allusion to the evidence on this subject.

Lord Sudeley, whose judgment cannot be questioned, said in his place in
the House of Peers: "The ventilation of the House of Commons was complete
and perfect—and the first plan of systematic ventilation ever carried out in
this or any other country." He also stated, in another document already
quoted, that "To the skill, zeal, and determination of Dr. Reid, it is owing that the
members of the House of Commons can now pursue their senatorial duties without
a sacrifice of either health or comfort. To him we owe the solution of the problem,
that, by a proper system, ventilation may be obtained in the most trying and difficult circumstances." Lord Sudeley, also, as Chairman of the Commissioners who
selected the design for the new Houses of Parliament, had the best means of
knowing the realities of Dr. Reid's plans, especially as he voluntarily acted as the
architect when these plans were executed at the temporary House of Commons. The House of Commons' Committee in 1846, ten years after they had
tested Dr. Reid's plans, reported, that; "The great improvement which Dr. Reid has
effected in the atmosphere of the existing House of Commons, can be appreciated
by every member of the House; and your Committee entirely concur in what they
consider to be the general opinion in its favour."—*Extract from the Report of the
Committee of the House of Commons*, presented on the 5th of August, 1846.

The Chairman of the Committee on Acoustics and Ventilation, Sir Benjamin
Hawes, in 1835, used the following language, after the House had fully tried the plans,
viz., "You have facilitated public business, and prolonged the lives of public men."

The Queen's Physician, Sir James Clarke, stated in 1843, that "Dr. Reid's success in the ventilation of the Houses of Parliament, and similar efforts in the same.

In the plans applied at the temporary House of Commons, the utmost care was taken in selecting a supply of fresh air from the least objectionable source. It was even washed, screened, and treated with chemicals, when loaded with the dense soot of a November atmosphere in London, or with noxious emanations from neighboring manufactories; while the drains and sewers in the immediate vicinity, were subjected to a special power that withdrew all offensive gases and vapors. Further, the whole ground in the vicinity was treated with caustic lime or other chemicals, wherever it exhaled an offensive smell. In the House itself the temperature, moisture, and movement of the air were adapted to the ever-varying attendance, and the state of the weather, with a power that would give one foot or 50,000 cubic feet of air, at pleasure, per minute, or any intermediate proportion, according to the necessities of the case. The whole arrangements for previous preparation, management, and control, were placed on a systematic footing that had never before been contemplated. The windows were not opened, even for a single occasion, during the fifteen years it was in operation, from 1836 to 1851, and the surface of diffusion given to the entering air exceeded, in the body of the House alone, 4,000 feet. The air, vitiated in the lower part of the House, was never permitted to contaminate the separate supply given to the galleries. The products of combustion from lamps and candles, as well as respiration, were all removed as they were formed, and never permitted to return within the zone of respiration.

Three years after the introduction of Dr. Reid's plans in the House of Commons, the House of Peers, in a public debate, pressed upon Government the importance of some measures being taken for the relief of their House, referring to the comfort of the House of Commons; but

direction, would do more to improve the public health than any measure with which he was acquainted."

In his evidence before the House of Commons' Committee of 1852, Dr. Neil Arnott stated: "Until the late House of Commons existed as ventilated by Dr. Reid, there never was in the world a room in which 500 persons or more could sit for ten hours in the day, and day after day, for long periods, not only with perfect security to health, but with singular comfort. I think," says Dr. Arnott, "an important novelty was therein achieved."

they did not vote one-fifth of the means which had been applied to the former House. The measures introduced were consequently of a much more limited nature ; but such as they were, the satisfaction they gave was equally admitted by the separate administrations under Lord Melbourne and Sir Robert Peel ; the former presenting to Parliament, in 1841, on the occasion of the introduction of Dr. Reid's plans for the new Houses, a document written by the Earl of Besborough, a member of the preceding Cabinet, in which he referred to the general satisfaction which these partial improvements had given.

The plans for the new Houses of Parliament were projected on a magnificent scale, and were afterwards combined with an improved system of warming, lighting, and ventilating, founded on Dr. Reid's experiments at Edinburgh and other places, in unison with the recommendation of Government and of Parliamentary Committees. The plans of Mr. Barry (afterwards Sir Charles Barry), were selected from the numerous designs presented for the new buildings, and Mr. Barry was appointed architect under the authority of the Commissioners of her Majesty's Woods and Forests, of whom Lord Besborough was chief. The services of Dr. Reid being demanded by his government, he was called to London to superintend the ventilation of the new Houses, and required to reside permanently at the capital until the completion of the works. This being an honorable and an important service, affording, as it did, a most favorable opportunity for illustrating highly important principles in ventilation and the laws of domiciliary health, Dr. Reid accepted the call, relinquished his varied labors at Edinburgh, removed to London, and entered upon the duties of his appointment.

But Dr. Reid's experience at the new Houses of Parliament affords a memorable example of the difficulties attending the introduction of improvements, even when their practicability and success have been sufficiently demonstrated, when an inventor has to co-operate with another, who has the power of construction in his hands, and who has also the means of opposition, and of sheltering such opposition under the undefinable limits of taste and decoration.*

---

* Not only were the original plans altered from time to time, in numerous respects, by proper authority ; but Dr. Reid has given testimony that the central

As the new edifice progressed, it became evident that without a fair spirit of co-operation on the part of the architect, every essential provision in Dr. Reid's plans for ventilation might be seriously embarrassed or utterly frustrated. We do not propose to enter upon an examination of the merits of questions and dissensions so long at issue between Sir Charles Barry, the Commissioners, and Dr. Reid. Those who will investigate the subject can find ample documentary evidence of the fact that while, in the temporary House of Commons, where Dr. Reid had unrestricted authority in *executing* the works for the ventilation, remarkably satisfactory results were secured, even during the most crowded sessions; at the new Houses, the plans and works for the ventilation were so unreasonably thwarted by the architect, that it became the duty of Dr. Reid to protest against the injurious interference to which the more essential provisions and features of his plans were continually, unnecessarily, and capriciously subjected.

It should be mentioned to their honor, that the House of Commons continued to sustain Dr. Reid's position and plans. Powerful as were the efforts made, by interested parties, against the plans for ventilation, and vacillating as was the policy pursued in the works of construction; the public investigation, which Dr. Reid at last obtained, of the history of his relations to those works, and the final results of the arbitration, most triumphantly sustained him,* and gave a release from duties,

---

ventilating tower, the flues in connection and the chamber below it, the chambers under the House of Peers and the House of Commons, the flues in the roof, and many other places, were so altered by the architect, without authority, that Dr. Reid resolved at last to lay the matter before the Commissioners; having determined to cast off all responsibility unless proper arrangements were made in future for controlling the proceedings of the architect.

* Seven years previous to this arbitration the architect attacked Dr. Reid with counter charges, which he utterly rejected and opposed. Inquiries were then instituted, and in the following year a Committee of the House of Commons, of which Lord John Russell and Lord Palmerston were members, took up the question, and after examining both the architect and Dr. Reid, as well as the Commissioners and the referee of the preceding year, recommended unanimously to the House a resolution that met the difficulties of the case, and gave both Dr. Reid and Sir Charles Barry the power to nominate arbiters for deciding on every point on which they differed.

which, for several years, had partially diverted him from the grand purpose of his life, viz. the instruction of the people in the science and arts of daily life, based on the principles and practice of Chemistry.

But the labors of that Committee were rendered nugatory by the proceedings of the Marquis of Clanricarde, who succeeded in persuading the Peers to isolate their House from the plans that had been carried on for six years on the works, though the chairman of the Commissioners who selected the design for the new Houses, the Duke of Wellington, and the present Lord Chief-Justice of the Queen's Bench (Lord Campbell), opposed this measure, and pointed out the importance of the two Houses —Peers and Commons—coming to some mutual understanding on the subject, instead of taking opposite courses, and thus doing an act of injustice to Dr. Reid. The Government, perplexed by the novelty and peculiarities of the case, threw themselves into the hands of the architect.

Many weeks had not elapsed, however, before they appear to have repented of this step, for they restored the most important part of the building to Dr. Reid, viz. the House of Commons, and requested from him a special plan to suit the altered circumstances of the case.

But Dr. Reid had so deep a sense of the injustice done to him in the House of Peers, by the Marquis of Clanricarde, and of the impossibility of his plan having any fair play unless the architect was controlled as the House of Commons had specified, that he never acted again at the Houses of Parliament except under protest. He constantly demanded investigation; and six years afterwards he obtained a majority of more than two to one against the Government, in a vote that called him to the bar; where he pointed out, before the whole House, the utter impossibility of their having any comfortable atmosphere in their new House till the unnecessary injuries done to his plans by the architect were remedied. No man could deny what was thus brought so publicly before the House. Dr. Reid's evidence was printed and distributed next morning, with the printed official proceedings, to all the members. The Government and the House, by a Committee, immediately supported him in an entire change of the system of lighting; and empowered him, in addition to other works adopted during its sitting, to execute no less than thirty-five recommendations which he afterwards made. In the same year, Lord Derby's Government, which had in the meantime come into power, gave him an arbitration that necessarily secured the investigation he had so long in vain demanded, not as a favor but as a right. At this arbitration, Dr. Reid insisted on his right to cross-examine the architect, and such was the force and character of the evidence elicited, that the arbiters sustained Dr. Reid for seven successive days in pursuing this cross-examination; and they took evidence altogether on thirty different days. Their decision awarded Dr. Reid £3250 in addition to the sum of £4400, paid to

The magnificent pile of buildings, stretching for nearly the fifth of a mile on the banks of the Thames, though yet remaining unfinished, even after an incessant draft upon the national treasury for a period of twenty years, and after innumerable modifications, still bears too much of the impress of Dr. Reid's plans in its walls, its roof, its vaults, and its finishings, ever to be severed from its association with his labors; nor can those who may now, or hereafter direct the ventilation, deviate materially from the data he developed, without infringing on the laws of health and misinterpreting the principles of physical science. Dr. Reid's Central Ventilating Tower may indeed be truncated and curtailed of its fair proportions, but new and minor turrets make up the necessary equivalent, and corresponding alterations in the interior works can readily be met by proportionate arrangements.

It was not in vain, however, that Dr. Reid relinquished his favorite field of labors at Edinburgh, for such a service as that which he accepted. During the period of his residence at London, he enjoyed the most favorable opportunities for awakening an interest, not only on the subject of improved ventilation, but he was enabled also to advocate, in the most practical manner, a vast number of questions connected with improvements in domiciliary life and the public health. He was called to execute works for improved ventilation in various public buildings, and the influence of his executed works is now enjoyed throughout Europe and in our own country. In hospitals, asylums, court rooms, prisons, workshops, churches, and royal residences, Dr. Reid's plans

him as salary during the six years that he had constantly refused to act except under protest. They refused to give him any award on claims which the state of the law did not permit them to authorize. Sir John Forbes, however, one of the two arbiters, subsequently gave Dr. Reid a written statement with full authority to publish it, that the deed of arbitration had been so worded by the legal authorities employed by the Board of Works as not to permit fairness or justice in the popular sense of the term, but only such a decision as a court of law or equity could permit. He states: "Had I felt myself justified by the deed of arbitration to come to a decision on grounds of moral justice or fairness only, as in case of difference between man and man, I would have given my voice for an award greatly beyond the sum actually adjudged."

have been extensively adopted in a greater or a less degree, and with the happiest results. A distinguished architect, who has introduced the plans of Dr. Reid in the construction of forty-eight public and private edifices, erected under his own supervision, testifies that "the continued use of the scheme of ventilation proposed by Dr. Reid, gives daily increasing satisfaction."

In 1852, Mr. Thomas Brown of Edinburgh, as member of the Committee for Improvement of Prisons, when examined as to Dr. Reid's plans, by a committee of the House of Commons, stated, " I find every day that the more I attend to carrying out the views which he originally suggested to me, when fair opportunities occur, the better I succeed. We introduce his system from prison to prison as we go on."

In the ventilation of hospitals, vast improvements have been effected, some good examples of which exist in our own country. The present improved system of ventilation and warming in the New York City Hospital, is considered the best that has been put in operation in any large establishment in this city, though the ventilation in that institution is manifestly susceptible of vast improvements.

The beneficial results of a *perfect* system of ventilation in hospitals have been happily illustrated in a large hospital at Copenhagen, where, as mentioned by Dr. Channing of Boston, a case of fever did not occur for years after Dr. Reid's system of ventilation was introduced, though previously the infection of deadly fevers had been persistent.

The history of the Lambeth Hospital, London, strikingly illustrates the same point. A physician stated before the Health of Towns Commission, that, " The hospital was seldom free, for any length of time, from fever, occasionally producing frightful ravages, and requiring the building every now and then to be closed. After the greatest attention had been paid to cleanliness in every respect, the wards left open night and day for weeks, fumigated, the walls limed and painted, the beds thoroughly cleaned, fumigated, repaired, and frequently renewed, and the most scrupulous attention paid to cleanliness, the fever re-appeared, on some occasions, *immediately* on the hospital being re-opened." External causes were sought for, and more than $2,500 was expended in improving and covering drains, etc., in the vicinity. Dr. Rigby, the physician, states that " fever still continued to make its appearance from time to time, and occasionally with great severity. * * * * The air of the wards was always close, oppressive, and bedroomy, which I can only attribute to want of proper ventilation. * * As soon as Dr. Reid's plan of ventilation was permitted to have a fair trial, the air in the wards became not merely free from effluvia, but has now a remarkably clean, clear, refreshing feel, which I can only compare to the sensation produced on entering an empty room which has been recently whitewashed." (See *First Report of the Commissioners for inquiring into the State of Large Towns and Popular Districts*, p. 412.)

Since this important improvement was effected in the ventilation of that establishment, the fatal fevers, previously indigenous there, have scarcely been experienced in the wards, except as the direct and immediate result of suspending the use of the ventilating apparatus. The latest accounts we have from that hospital, are given in a paper read by Dr. Bence Jones at the Royal Institution in London, where, it is shown by statistical details, that the mortality there had been very greatly reduced by means of the improved ventilation, and that it increased whenever the ventilation was suspended.

Similar results have been experienced in all public institutions where improved ventilation has been introduced, and that, in exact proportion to the degree of improvement secured.

The following items, connected with miscellaneous works executed by Dr. Reid, will give some idea of the want of adequate ventilation in different classes of buildings, before his plans came into operation.

At the Chapel Royal, St. James's Palace, London, the ventilation was entirely recast; the supply of air largely increased; means of heat provided; allowing a great reduction of its intensity. A cooling chamber for warm weather was also provided, together with a metallic ventilating shaft about five feet in diameter, the action of which was secured by heat.

At Windsor Castle, a special ventilating shaft was constructed for the dining-room most frequently in use, and minor branches from some contiguous rooms were led into it.

At Buckingham Palace there was no outlet for vitiated air from several of the principal state apartments, exceeding a foot in area, exclusive of doors and windows, until Dr. Reid constructed a shaft of *twenty-seven feet in area*, within which a very powerful gas burner was introduced. At the same time, many other subsidiary arrangements were made, and the whole of the vitiated air from the basement, that had previously inundated the state apartments, was diverted by turning a minor staircase into a separate discharging shaft.

At the Old Bailey, referred to on page x, the theatre of so many criminal trials in the heart of the metropolis, as well as the scene of many sanitary investigations, both in the present and preceding buildings; enormous quantities of waste materials, principally wood, in a state of decomposition, were removed; a tunnel excavated, having *an area of fifty feet*, for the supply of air to the principal chambers and offices; and a steam engine of ten-horse power erected for driving a large fanner that supplied fresh air.

In numerous other Law Courts great improvements were also made. At the Opera House, in London, the only discharge for vitiated air, exclusive of doors and windows, was a tube of *two feet diameter*. This was replaced by a discharge having *seventy-five feet area*.

In no other places were greater evils pointed out than in churches, schools, and prisons. The galleries of some churches, although frequently crowded with children from asylums, received no air but the vitiated atmosphere that ascended from the body of the church. In answer to inquiries, the reply was that they were often sick. Some school rooms intended for a certain number of children, were often crowded with ten times that number; and in prisons no systematic power was applied for the removal of vitiated air. In all works of this description, leading channels were provided for the ingress and egress of air, and a *ventilating shaft, or other moving power, introduced so as to secure the ventilation whatever might be the state of the weather. The area of supply often exceeded by fifty times or upwards that formerly provided, while the power secured for extreme cases still more largely augmented the supply of air.* In different manufactories in towns and populous districts, peculiar arrangements, as exemplified in the last six figures in this volume, were adopted both for the health of the workmen and for the protection of the public. Among the arrangements that had preceded Dr. Reid's labors, nothing had contributed more in many establishments to the purity of the air, than the local use of fanners and flues for the removal of dust. To the imperial Russian works at Alexandroski, near St. Petersburgh, plans and apparatus were forwarded for the Chemical Schools there, at the request of government. The Tuileries and the Palais Royal in Paris were officially examined and reported on by Dr. Reid; and as is usually the case in places of such public assemblage, the supply of fresh air was found utterly inadequate for health, and the escape of vitiated air so imperfectly provided for, that at great receptions, the combustion of the candles and other lights was frequently interfered with by the extreme impurity of the air on such occasions.

At the Lambeth Maternity Hospital, the wards were for a protracted period so ravaged by the fatal fevers peculiar to such institutions, that it was often necessary to close the establishment; but when Dr. Reid's plans for ventilation were introduced, at once the sanitary condition of the wards was put on a new footing. The fatal miasma of fever was dissipated, and health was restored to the hospital.

Finally, we may with confidence refer to the condition of the ventilation in the British Halls of Legislation previously to the year 1836. We will quote the language of Lord Sudeley, writing subsequently to the introduction of Dr. Reid's plans :—" The pestilential atmosphere of the House of Commons was notorious; its baneful effects on the health and energies of the members were painfully felt and admitted : Means from time to time were resorted to, to correct the evil, till scarcely a hope remained, even that it could be lessened; and the most sanguine never dreamt that it could be cured; much less that the ventilation of the Houses could be brought to such a degree of perfection, as to defy the chills of winter and the heat of summer, or the effects of numbers, however great, congregated within the walls, lessening its beneficial effects."

In naval architecture, the same general deficiency existed respecting ventilation, that had engaged attention on shore. Notwithstanding the intense interest experienced in Great Britain, in consequence of terrible mortality on board naval and prison ships; and at a later day, the heart-sickening fatality from lack of ventilation in emigrant passenger vessels; and though the causes of such disastrous mortality had been investigated and strongly urged upon the attention of government by Dr. Lind and Sir Gilbert Blane; and all the ingenuity of Desaguliers, Sutton, and Hales had been exercised in the device of means for remedying such evils, no adequate and permanent impression has yet been produced among the great mass of directors of construction, either in the government or mercantile marine.

Until Dr. Reid's plans were applied in the three ships of the Niger Expedition, and in the Queen's Yacht, "Victoria and Albert," there was no example of any ship that had a system of ventilating channels constructed and applied to every compartment in the ship, and capable of being made to act on every portion at the same time, or on any of them individually, with a power that could be rendered at all times efficient.

In the "Minden"—the Hospital Ship sent by the government for the relief of the troops who suffered much during the former Chinese war, very ample provision was made for ventilation; and in the Yacht "Royal George," a sailing vessel in which the Queen made her first trip to Scotland, Dr. Reid introduced a ventilating screw fanner, which was made to operate on the principal apartments.*

* The Rt. Hon. L. Corry, the Secretary of the Admiralty in 1845, in an official communication to Dr. Reid, makes the following statement:—

"I am commanded by my Lords Commissioners of the Admiralty to acquaint you, that it appears from a report made upon your ventilating apparatus fitted in the Royal Yacht, that its operations were quite perfect. The exhaustion of vitiated air, and the supply of fresh air being easily regulated by the occupant of each apartment, and the apparatus being sufficiently powerful to keep up the necessary change in all the apartments, while at the same time the whole power of the machine can be thrown upon one apartment."

The late Mr. Creuze, F.R.S., Naval Architect of H.M. Dockyard, Portsmouth, Author of a Treatise on Naval Architecture, and of the Article, "Naval Architecture," in the Encyclopædia Britannica, recorded his opinion in the following terms:—

"I have had the pleasure of working in conjunction with Dr. Reid in the *practical application* of your admirable system of ventilation to H.M. Navy, and I can bear testimony as to the unqualified approval your proposals met with from the Committee which was appointed by the Admiralty to investigate them."

Dr. McWilliam, now surgeon to H.M. Customs, at London, and senior medical offi-

The improvement of ventilation in all classes of vessels employed in the transportation of passengers, is manifestly of no less importance than the proper ventilation of dwellings on land; and we trust that the subject will soon receive that attention which its acknowledged value demands. Not only the health, but the lives also of those who traverse the sea and our inland waters, are jeopardised in consequence of the bad ventilation of ships and steam-vessels. Indeed, facts warrant the assertion that a greater number of lives are annually sacrificed by this easily removable cause, than by disasters at sea and the terrible accidents on our lakes and rivers. In addition to this, it should be stated, that were ample ventilation secured on shipboard, a vessel at sea would be one of the most healthful of human habitations; while under such conditions the importation of any form of transmissible infection would be rendered next to impossible.

We might multiply examples of varied character in illustration of

cer of the Niger Expedition, in his valuable work giving the history of that expedition, states,—"The system of ventilation adopted in the vessels of the Niger Expedition, according to the plans proposed by Dr. Reid, presented the first systematic attempt that had been made to place every compartment of a ship under the immediate and direct control of a ventilating power." And though it did not cure the malarious atmosphere, and prevent those fatal results that arose when they plunged into one of the districts of Western Africa most noted for malignant fevers, there is abundant evidence both in Dr. McWilliam's interesting account, and other reports, that it must have produced beneficial results, and diminished the severity of the sufferings which the Expedition encountered.

Dr. Wilson, another British Naval Officer, in his Medical Notes on China, states, in reference to Dr. Reid's plans for the ventilation of the Minden, a seventy-four gun ship at Hong Kong, and fitted up in England as an hospital ship,—"The machinery was simple and did its work well—that, namely, of moving the air briskly and diffusively in any or every part of the hospital, as was desired, the force being less or more, in relation to the space to which it was applied."

Mr. Chatfield, Naval Architect, in a communication addressed to Dr. Reid, also states,—"The efficiency of your ventilating apparatus, as fitted on board the 'Minden' hospital ship by me, according to your views and instructions, was most perfect, and delighted every one." And he adds, "I cannot but feel anxious that you should be enabled to extend your principle of ventilation to our navy generally, under any circumstances in which you may be placed."

the vast importance of complete ventilation in all apartments and edifices where large numbers of persons are assembled, particularly in hospitals, asylums, churches, schools, and manufactories; but it is not the object of the present work to enter upon those topics, except as they may serve to elucidate the practical utility and importance of the suggestions made by Dr. Reid in this volume. We would, however, refer to Dr. Reid's "*Illustrations of Ventilation*," published by Messrs. Longman of London, as well as to the following pages.

In conclusion, we desire to invite the public mind to an attentive consideration of the principles and examples of ventilation presented in this volume; their vast importance cannot fail to be generally acknowledged, while they will be found capable of almost universal application, and well adapted to promote personal health and the comforts of domestic life.

ELISHA HARRIS, M.D.

NEW YORK, March 4, 1858.

IMPROVEMENT OF VENTILATION

IN

AMERICAN DWELLINGS.

CHAPTER I.

INTRODUCTION.

FEW practical questions are more important to man than the construction and condition of the habitation in which he dwells, and its right adaptation to his moral, physical, and social wants.

In the mansions of the opulent as well as in the abodes of the poor all equally require shelter from the inclemency of the weather, proper opportunities of rest, refreshment, and recreation, and that attention to the structure of the human frame which shall prevent them from impeding its natural functions and laying the foundation of disease.

It is not too much to affirm that the average duration of human life might at least be largely increased with the attendant blessings which this usually implies, were habitations more generally built, and cities and villages more largely provided with those resources which health and comfort equally demand.

In proportion as the extension of civilization and the multiplication of arts and manufactures increases man's natural wants, and he departs from the simplicity, habits, food, and exercise which a more primitive state of society presents, the more essential is it for him that his dwelling shall not interfere with the free operation of those laws that regulate the functions of the human frame.

The tendency to crowd in large cities, to occupations that give too little bodily exercise, or that are accompanied by an unequal strain on some individual organ, particularly if that be the brain, and the exposure of the whole system to the contaminating impurities arising from a vitiated atmosphere, multiplies the danger from this source. On the other hand, improved drainage, better supplies of water, and more comfortable habitations diminish the tendency to disease and death.

In these pages we have to deal with special physical agents that affect life, and restricting our observations accordingly, let it be remembered that there is not to be seen, in all the visible works of creation with which man is acquainted, one more marvellously perfect, or more wonderfully adjusted in its varied ramifications, than that which conveys fresh air to the lungs in the living system by the process of respiration, and circulates the regenerated blood to every fibre of the body in a never-ceasing stream. The chest rises and falls with upwards of a thousand respirations per hour during the whole period of existence, while millions of air-cells purify the minutest particles of the blood, and the heart beats several thousand times an hour in maintaining that perpetual circulation of the vital fluid through an infinite number of arteries, veins, and other vessels, without which we could neither see, nor hear, nor feel, nor could any organ or tissue exercise its appropriate functions.

But all these provisions are more or less frustrated or impaired, whenever there is a bad external atmosphere, or a defective internal supply to the habitations of the people, or in any other place or building which they may frequent.

Without this purification of the blood by the air, unwholesome currents permeate the system, oppress the brain, break out into disease, and terminate too often fatally by scrofula, consumption, or fever that may long prey upon the system when the state of the atmosphere is not so extreme as to cause immediate death. Let this admitted fact be realized to its full extent, and the misery, suffering, and loss attendant on it. Let the magnitude of the provisions be fully considered by which health is sustained when not counteracted by the artificial impediments which want of information and inattention may oppose to them.

In Europe the sanitary question has assumed so much importance that it has largely engaged the attention of the different governments, and enlisted the co-operation of all classes of society. In many examples, however, bad ventilation is accompanied with other evils, moral, social, and physical, that greatly aggravate its effects; and where they are combined with poverty and vice, pictures of degradation and misery are presented which, though long known to professional men, cannot be said to have widely awakened the sympathies of their more prosperous neighbors, till the progress of " Illustrated Works " and periodicals have presented scenes and unfolded realities that have aroused public attention to the condition of the masses of the population.

In the United States the importance is no less urgent, and its professional men have equally borne testimony to the magnitude of the question. The ordinary bills of mortality give a key to the condition of the population in this as well as in other respects.

The right supply of air being more continuously, if not more imperiously, called for than any other provision which life demands, ventilation is necessarily a question of prime necessity. It is one of the most important objects of hygiene, and should be deemed an essential, and not a mere secondary question in all architectural structures.

If it should be asked why so much attention is directed to ventilation in modern times, it is sufficient to reply that the progress of art has led in these later days to the construction of habitations that are much more air-tight than the dwellings of former times; to the introduction of a more brilliant system of internal lighting, or illumination; to the use of powerful stoves and other heating apparatus; to the exclusion of open fire-places; to occupations affecting largely the quality of the air within doors, as well as in mines, ships, and manufactories, where the system is often exposed to deleterious gases and vapors unknown in ancient days. All these circumstances, as well as the increasing density of the population in numerous cities, and the knowledge which science has unfolded of the nature and relation of the air and other gases to the human frame, have equally developed the sources of numerous evils that prey upon human life, and pointed out the means by which they may be obviated. Where superstition and want of information too often attributed many sources of sickness and plague to a supernatural agency, they are now more generally and correctly ascribed to the neglect of those laws which a divine providence has instituted, and of those warnings which are given by the senses, when their perceptions are not blunted by a too long and continuous exposure to noxious emanations.

An all wise and omnipotent Creator has placed at the disposal of man, for the present at least, the entire control and occupation of this globe, so far as he can render it amenable to his wants with the abilities given to him. Every day almost, in modern times, developes some new power, principle, or material, which he had previously overlooked, and adds to his means of occupation, direction, or enjoyment. But he has not as yet, generally speaking, become sufficiently sensible of the magnitude of the gift, and of the untold treasures which it still contains, to lead him to support the introduction of the study of the material world in his primary schools of instruction. When that is done with proper experimental illustrations, it will be reasonable to expect the awakening of the intelligence of the whole population, to the power and wonder of Creation. The medical profession will then be more thoroughly supported in their attempts to improve public Hygiene, and Architects will be more largely empowered to improve the ventilation of public and private buildings.

It is not often practicable to estimate precisely the relative amount of sickness and loss of life arising from the different causes that may concur in their production, but it would require a very moderate examination to demonstrate that the average duration of human life might at least be doubled, when no unusual circumstances occur to shorten it, by a proper and extended system of Hygiene. The history and interpretation by the most eminent biblical critics of the passage in the nine-tieth psalm,* which has originated a prevailing popular belief that the years of man have been, by a divine ordinance, reduced to three-score and ten, do not bear out this opinion. Statistical records have shown how often it is largely exceeded, though the present average is much below this standard; and

* Some of the most learned commentators consider that this psalm was written by Moses.

that it may be more correctly translated as a lamentation, that at a special period during the wandering of the Israelites, human life was reduced to that period, from the suffering they endured.

By placing a money value upon human life, and on the losses from sickness and death arising from preventible causes, this question has been placed in bold relief, and it is perhaps not too much to assert that the pecuniary value of human life might probably be at least doubled, by a systematic attention to a right code of hygienic laws. As it is at present, how many are there who appear as if they were merely born to die after five or ten years of a painful and harassing childhood, to say nothing of valuable lives cut off in their prime!

Among recent examples of loss arising from a defective state of the atmosphere in ships, the amount expended on Quarantine last year, directly and indirectly in New York, has been estimated at a million of dollars. Had the ships detained, been ventilated previously, and more attention paid in drying some cargoes before shipping them, a very small part of the expense would have been incurred.

Were the details of individual cases in different classes of buildings given, they would embrace every variety of effect, from the slightest headache produced by an indifferent atmosphere, to examples of hospitals where no patient ever survived an operation; and there the pestilential air, sometimes oppressing the patient much more than the disease by which he had been attacked, has led to his supposed death and removal to the dead-room, where the free play of an open atmosphere revived the apparent corpse and led to an ultimate recovery.

In the late memorable example of disease that occurred at the National Hotel, at Washington, very decisive testimony was given that the state of the atmosphere there had at least a most important share in its production; that cases of sudden and severe vomiting occurred where the bad air was most abundant; and that, had the representations made on this subject been acted upon before those extreme results arose that led finally to the closing of the hotel, all complaints from this source would have been avoided.* The loss to the proprietors in closing a large hotel must have been very considerable; and the number of cases of illness, estimated at upwards of seven hundred, if the report be correct, must have entailed a large additional expense on individuals, to say nothing of loss of time, or of those cases of death that have been attributed to this cause.

If individual habitations be made the object of attention, it will be found that there are few in which some of the inmates do not experience annually some loss from evils arising from the imperfect attention given to the subject of ventilation. In different places in England, where many details have been entered into on this subject, with the records available in various cities and rural districts, it is considered that the expense from preventible causes that would disappear with the introduction of right sanitary measures, is rarely less than a pound per head annually, however much it may exceed that sum. This would give about five millions of dollars annually for New York and the cities adjoining it, should they be estimated by a similar standard; and it may be affirmed that bad ventilation, directly or indirectly, from imperfect drainage and cleansing, is the principal item in all such calculations. New York has numerous natural advantages from its position that

* Whether its effects may or may not have been increased by other causes and their proportionate influence, is another question.

give it a great superiority in many respects, and a supply and quality of water from the Croton works that cannot be too highly prized, and far beyond any that can be found in European cities with a similar population. The severity of the winter's cold, however, and of the summer's heat, which, with the peculiarities of its soil and rocks, render it prone to accumulate offensive waters in many places not yet filled up nor drained artificially, as well as the extent to which gas is used, and imperfections in ventilation, perhaps balance its advantages. Were they not neutralized to a considerable extent by such and similar causes, New York should show bills of mortality with which few large cities could compare; but the rapidity with which it has risen has not given time, as yet, to deal with all the difficulties which its foundations present, and to take advantage of all the opportunities which its site affords. In no great city, probably, has so much ever been accomplished in a similar period, particularly if the provisions for future extension be taken in connexion with existing arrangements. Local drainage and a right system of cleansing are the great desiderata, and the proper application of the refuse to agricultural purposes, as a means of defraying the necessary expenses.

Though it is in large cities that the most extreme results are usually observed, they are by no means confined to such localities; and accordingly in villages and in isolated habitations, long continued indifference or neglect may induce parallel evils. The united co-operation of Medical men, Architects, Engineers, and Agriculturists, is required to place the sanitary question on a right footing in town and country, however much may be done to improve internal ventilation in each individual habitation.

CHAPTER II.

EXPLANATORY REMARKS.

IN perusing the following pages, the accompanying summary will facilitate the examination of the varied examples they present, and of the leading objects they are intended to illustrate.

The actual amount of air respired by an adult is not considered to exceed a quarter of a cubic foot per minute, but the amount necessary for satisfactory ventilation greatly exceeds this estimate, as allowance must be made for the exhalations from the surface of the body, the influence of furniture, clothing, and the contamination of fresh air by the vitiated air expired, as well as the effect of lights, stoves, fire-places, and any other special cause in removing fresh air, or adding to the impurities of respiration. Hence a great difference in the estimates given by different authors and experimenters.

It is contended that ten cubic feet of air per minute forms an average supply, that is generally agreeable, though in cold weather with a dry atmosphere, and fresh air admitted and discharged under favorable circumstances, an amount varying from two to five cubic feet will be found sufficient. The condensation of the moisture of the breath by cold is in itself a powerful assistance to ventilation where the temperature is very low, variable quantities of carbonic acid and animal exhalations accompanying the moisture. On the other hand,

with a summer temperature, a much larger amount of ventilation is agreeable. A brisk current in the open air is
refreshing. With all the windows and doors open, there is
no complaint of too much air, till the temperature becomes
excessive; and then its movement must be reduced, and
warm air excluded as much as possible, within certain limits,
as well as the direct rays of the sun, and the reflection from
the vicinity.

The greater the changes in the external atmosphere, the
more varied must the provisions for ventilation be, and hence
with all the resources that doors and windows afford, in every
climate subject to extreme temperatures, there should also be
arrangements for removing vitiated air, warming cold, and
cooling warm air, in proportion to the severity of the seasons.
Without such means the best systematic ventilation cannot
be secured.

But without attempting in the majority of cases to secure
the most perfect arrangements, much may be done by simple
means to provide for the more pressing necessities of individual habitations where the ventilation is defective by the
following measures.

1. The adoption of measures for breaking the first and
harsh impulse of a cold raw atmosphere, by causing it to
enter with a gentle diffusion, or at a place where it necessarily
spreads over a much larger space before it comes in contact
with the person.

2. The more extended use of entrances, staircases, and
passages, for the supply of air to individual rooms, so as to
give an interior and milder climate within the house when
there is severe heat or cold externally.

3. The disposition of all kinds of heating apparatus, and

flues connected with them, so that they shall warm the floor of apartments as much as possible, either by the direct communication of heat to as large a part of the floor as can be conveniently appropriated for this purpose, or by the induction of rotatory currents and radiations that produce an equivalent effect. Nothing is so common where powerful heaters are employed, as great heat at the ceiling and a very uncomfortable, cold atmosphere at the level of the floor.

4. The communication of more moisture to the air than is usually given to it in very cold weather.

5. The reduction of the temperature at which stoves or heaters are generally used, and the compensation of any subsequent loss of power by a larger stove surface, so as to give a greater volume of air not so highly heated. This is a point to which great importance is attached. The imperative necessity of heat preceding the nature of the source from which it is obtained, it must be freely admitted that in numerous cases the present structure of flues and buildings will often prevent the necessary alterations being made for this purpose except at considerable expense. But there are few cases where much cannot be done to mitigate extreme effects by warming passages and a right adjustment between them and individual rooms. It should be laid down as an axiom in house building that no entrance, staircase, or passage, should be built so large, or in such a manner, that the tenant or proprietor should ever hesitate as to the importance of warming it, moderately at least, in winter. He should, in short, find as much or more economy in warming it, than in the expenditure of any of the fuel provided for winter use.

6. The direct removal of vitiated air from gas lamps or other sources of excessive illumination, and from products of

respiration. This is a very large question in some respects, however simple it may at first appear, and involves not merely the
removal of the products referred to, but also the consideration
of the supply of air; for in all rooms heated by flues leading in
warm air, and by stoves, hot water or steam pipes placed in
the individual rooms, the warmest air immediately ascends to
the ceiling, and there it will escape as in well ventilated and
crowded public buildings in proportion to the area of discharge, and the amount of supply, *without inducing those
rotatory currents on which the economy of warming such apartments principally depends.* Hence it is obvious that if air
could be more generally introduced over an extensive surface
at the ceiling in apartments in ordinary habitations, and the
vitiated air drawn to a central part there for escape by a ventilating flue, air might be permitted to enter at a less elevated
temperature, the rotatory currents and freshness of the atmosphere would be unimpaired, and a great economy would be
attained in the amount of fuel required. The colder the
winter the greater the facility and importance of such
arrangements, and of the transfer of part of the heat escaping with the bad air to the pure air as it enters, not by
direct contact but by conduction and radiation between the
materials of which the ceiling is composed.

7. The purification of the external atmosphere in the immediate vicinity of dwellings by improvements in cleansing,
drainage, closets, and the control of noxious vapors and gases
from manufactories.

. These seven points afford perhaps the most extended fields
for the improvement of ventilation, the economy of heat, and
the adaptation of designs in the construction of new buildings.
To them may be added improvements in windows and in the

open fireplace, in the means for supplying a cool atmosphere in oppressive summer weather, the construction of a special ventilating flue, and the use of valves adjusted to every aperture for the ingress or egress of air.

There is another point that requires much attention, and without which no adjustments for ventilation can be expected to give any satisfaction, and that is a reasonable view of all that ventilation may and may not be expected to accomplish. Where there is a great difference in constitution, temperament, and habits, different individuals can never expect to be equally satisfied with the same amount of ventilation or quality of atmosphere; there must be a mutual concession on such points, or special provisions introduced where individuals widely opposed to each other in these respects occupy the same apartment. It is one of the great advantages of an open fireplace, and of all radiators, that they permit such adjustments to be made with great facility and satisfaction.

The very inequality of their action gives them this power of accommodation in perfection. The room warmed with an equal stove or other heat, however superior in many respects, can boast of no such perfection, to say nothing of the cheerful influence of a living fire.

In many of the diagrams used in the following pages pink and blue coloring are introduced to indicate good and bad air, great advantage having accrued from this system since it was introduced in reports prepared by the author for the British government, and freely used in some of those that appear in parliamentary papers; many of them have been quoted in the United States.

The following extracts are taken from one of these reports that was very extensively distributed, particularly among teachers and others interested in sanitary improvements, as it was considered that their services would be rendered eminently useful in laying, through their pupils, a broad foundation for the progress of sanitary improvement.

In old and new apartments, the ever-varying details of local structure, exclusive of constitutional peculiarities among the inmates, give an equally varying influence to apertures of the same size. As a general rule, however, it may be stated that, in a room from 12 to 14 feet square, occupied by from six to twelve persons—

a. An aperture of one foot area for the ingress of air, and one foot area for egress, may be considered sufficient in moderate weather, if they are favorably disposed for promoting the movement of air.

b. Apertures of three or four inches square will relieve such apartments of the most extreme stagnation. If such apertures work well, passing into, or near warm flues, they are as large as the majority of persons will tolerate in winter weather, unless the air be warmed previously and well diffused at its entrance.

c. In summer weather the opening of a window may be necessary to give the same amount of relief which the small aperture affords in winter.

d. The air, after being led into an apartment, cannot be too largely diffused, before becoming generally distributed through it.

e. A well-constructed fire-place flue should not exceed 9 by 4½ inches area, unless a much larger fire be required than is necessary for an apartment such as has been mentioned; it is presumed that smokeless fuel alone is used, if the flue be not straight; where circular flues are introduced, they may be made still smaller.

f. Valves in the chimney flue, and in the ventilating apertures, can alone secure the varying adjustments which the varying state of the constitution demands.

g. Where ventilation is sustained by forced measures, or by the continuous heat of a kitchen fire, or any equivalent arrangement introduced for the purpose, much smaller apertures are sufficient for the ingress and egress of air than are otherwise necessary; the continuity and power of action compensating for the smaller dimensions.

h. Flues and chambers for fresh air should always be so constructed as to admit of their being inspected and cleaned.

Tabular View of Circumstances affecting the Supply of Air necessary for different Individuals in any Apartment.

I. General.

    1. Climate.

    2. Season.

    8. Time of day.

    4. Condition of the external air.

        a. Temperature.

        b. Hygrometric state.

        c. Electric state.

        d. Direction or force of the wind.

II. Local.

    1. Natural position of the apartment under consideration.

        a. Aspect in reference to the rays of the sun.

        b. On a mountain ridge.

        c. In a valley.

        d. Proximity to the sea.

        e. Position in respect to any other collection of water, or moist surface including the nature of the emanations from it.

        f. Condition of the soil, and vegetation in the vicinity.

    2. State of the drainage, natural and artificial, especially if unventilated drains discharge vitiated air in the vicinity, or in the apartment occupied.

    8. Form of the building in which it is placed, particularly in so far as it is favorable or unfavorable to external ventilation.

    4. Influence of mechanical or chemical impurities from manufactories, or deficient cleansing.

    5. Position in towns in respect to smoke or prevailing winds.

    6. State of the cleansing, particularly as affected by supplies of water.

III. Special.

    1. Quality of air supplied from without.

    2. Mode of adjusting quantity supplied to varying circumstances requiring attention.

3. Treatment to which the air is subjected.
    a. Heating.
    b. Drying.
    c. Moistening.
    d. Purifying.
    e. Velocity of movement.
    f. Amount of diffusion at its ingress.
    g. Position at which vitiated air is withdrawn.

4. Peculiarities of apartment.
    a. Altitude.
    b. Materials of which it is built.
    c. Position of door and windows.
    d. Single or double windows, or glazing.
    e. Influence of furniture or other materials.
    f. Natural inclination of currents or eddies within the apartment.
    g. Mode of lighting.

5. Crowding.
    a. Numbers on a given space.
    b. Their position within or without the zone of each other's respiration.

IV. Personal.
    a. Condition of the system at the moment, particularly as exhaling to the external atmosphere, or absorbing from it a greater ratio than is compensated by exhalation.
    b. Temperament.
    c. State of health.
    d. Age.
    e. Habits.
    f. Nature of diet; time that may have elapsed since any refreshment may have been taken.
    g. Clothing.
    h. Exercise taken.
    k. Relative amount of pulmonary or cutaneous exhalation.*
    l. Previous exposure.

* Some individuals exhale almost exclusively by their lungs, while in others the pulmonary exhalation of moisture at least is altogether trifling, compared with what is discharged by the body.

V. Dependent on occupation, nature and amount of labor in professional engagements, trades, and in positions where peculiar emanations require to be
guarded against.

This department is so extensive that very leading considerations can alone be
included in the following summary.

a. Inequality of clothing, and use of non-porous clothing.

When the professional engagements, or other circumstances, lead to inequality of
clothing, particularly where wigs and gowns give unusual protection to the head
and the body generally, while the feet may be comparatively unprotected, it is
impracticable, in crowded assemblies, to place the ventilation on the best footing, both
for individuals in this position and for others not so circumstanced, unless special
arrangements be made to meet both cases.

Similar considerations apply in innumerable cases in the habitations of the poor
and the dwellings of the rich, modified by an endless diversity of details, but all
agreeing in the obstacles presented to ventilation by the imperfect protection of the
feet which the nature of the climate requires, where it is not obviated by the introduction of warm air, or the proper diffusion of cold air. Soldiers wearing brass or steel
helmets, large boots and gloves, and other non-porous or imperfectly porous clothing,
may be often seen suffused with perspiration on the face, the escape of which is so
much obstructed from other parts of the body. Cases of death are recorded where
non-porous clothing is still more largely used.

b. Extreme and rapid transitions of temperature.

These tell more severely upon many constitutions than almost any other cause.
While all persons are subject to such transitions in passing between the external air
and ordinary apartments, it is in chemical manufactures more especially that their
more severe operation is experienced. Common sailors are more exposed to extreme
transitions than other classes of persons, being often called to leave their hammocks
where they are surrounded by hot and vitiated air, and to expose themselves to the
most chilling blasts.

c. Mechanical impurities.

These are of very great variety, according as they proceed from the general atmosphere of any town or district, or from any special materials communicated to the air
in manufacturing operations. Those evolved in grinding metals and in making flour,
mill stones present extreme cases of the fatal results that ensue where effective ventilating arrangements are not adopted. The dust from vegetable and animal matters

is often highly offensive, but rarely so deleterious as in the examples now mentioned.

d. Chemical impurities.

These are by far the most abundant and frequent sources of impure air in ordinary apartments, in public buildings, in manufactories, and mines. The following list contains a notice of the more extreme cases in which suffering, special disease, or general bad health, are most apt to arise from chemical impurities:—

1. Mines charged excessively with variable quantities of carbonic acid, carburetted hydrogen, or smoke from gunpowder used in blasting.

2. Chemical manufactories or class rooms charged with deleterious gases, mercurial vapors, &c. &c. Workmen in chlorine manufactories sometimes fall down suddenly, as if they were shot, when a blast of strong chlorine overpowers them. The most severe convulsions are observed in sal ammoniac manufactories, where the workmen have been exposed to sulphuretted hydrogen gas in less quantities than are sufficient to induce immediate death.

3. Offices, shops, workshops, and other crowded apartments, where the sole or principal source of heat is derived from the products of respiration, and the combustion of gas.

4. Bake-houses, in which carbonic acid from the fermenting sponge, air from drains, heat from an underground oven, and vitiated products from gas lamps contribute to produce an oppressive and soporific atmosphere, that would prey still more heavily on the constitution were it not for the severity of the exercise which the bakers undergo.

5. Printing-offices, when there is an immoderate use of gas, low ceilings, and no means of heat except from the gas lamps and products of respiration.

6. Coffee-rooms in hotels, more particularly those commonly termed "The travellers' Room," when without ventilation, and immoderately supplied with gas.

7. Lodging-houses for the humblest classes.

8. Public kitchens and private kitchens in large establishments, where non-ventilated charcoal fires, bad air from drains, and local draught, though producing much disease, are rendered milder in their effects so long as ample diet does not derange the digestive functions.

9. Store-houses of volatile ingredients.

10. Grave-diggers, scavengers, and persons employed in cleaning drains, more especially when first engaged in such work, and before the constitution has, to a certain extent, been acclimated to it, suffer much from noxious emanations.

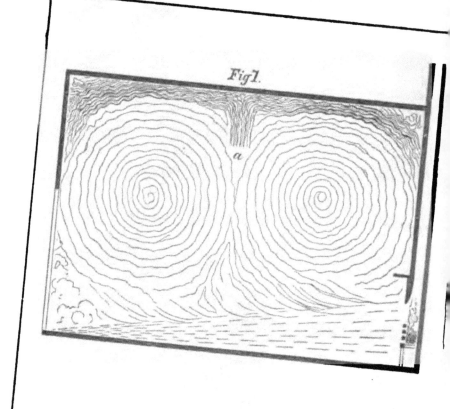

Fig. 1.

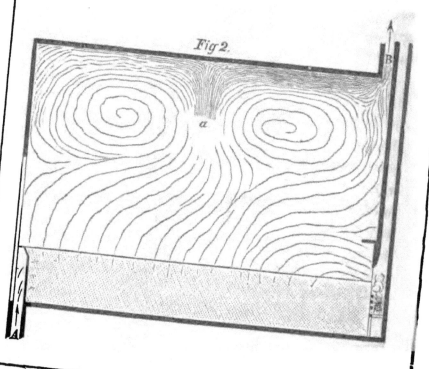

Fig. 2.

CHAPTER III.

VENTILATION OF A ROOM LOADED WITH PRODUCTS OF COMBUSTIC FROM GAS, AND SUBJECT TO OFFENSIVE COLD CURRENTS ON THE FLOOR.

In a room warmed by an open fire, there are great complaints of a current of cold air passing along the floor, while the air on the line of respiration feels heavy and oppressive, producing great restlessness, particularly when a series of gas-burners are lighted that give a brilliant illumination. This is one of the most common forms of complaint in numerous apartments, and the causes will be obvious on inspecting the accompanying figures.

The air admitted being very cold, and entering partly by a slight leakage at the window, but principally below the door, from a passage not warmed artificially, has little tendency to rise, and passes along the floor to the fire-place. The gas, however, induces a powerful current at *a*, Fig. 1, which ascends with force and strikes upon the ceiling, where it is soon diffused, and descends on every side as it cools. Part of it mixes with fresh air below, and is carried off by the action of the fire; the rest ascends again by a rotatory movement towards the gas-burners, where it mingles a second time in the current, ascending and descending as before. The upper portion of the air is accordingly largely charged with moisture and carbonic acid gas, the principal products of its combustion.

In Fig. 2, the principal arrangements necessary for removing these evils are shown in one of the many modes by which this can be accomplished.

A free supply of air is admitted by the flue A, being drawn from a central apparatus supplying warm air. A much smaller open fire is then sufficient; with warmer air it may be rendered unnecessary. In warm weather cold air is admitted by the flue A. It is not permitted to enter abruptly at one place, but diffused at the base-board by perforated zinc, or at a panel from which it escapes into the apartment to be supplied. A vitiated air flue, B, starting at the level of the ceiling, continuously removes the bad air, and preserves fresh air at and immediately above the zone of respiration, the great object in all ventilated apartments.

A reference to the succeeding diagrams will explain many modifications that may be adopted in carrying such alterations into effect.

The primary objects in all ventilation are the removal of vitiated air, and the introduction of fresh air in an imperceptible stream. The diffusion of the entering air in a chamber, air trunk, or channel, indicated by the deeper tint proceeding from A, Fig. 2, breaks its impetus in proportion to the extent of diffusion. The warmer the air supplied, and the more distant from A the portion of floor generally occupied, the less is the amount of diffusion required. The vitiated air may be discharged directly into the external atmosphere, or any of the arrangements may be adopted that are indicated in Chapters IV and V.

CHAPTER IV.

SPECIAL VENTILATING FLUE.

THE introduction of a special ventilating flue being recommended as an auxiliary to the present arrangements in ordinary use for the purpose of ventilation, it will be necessary to explain the principal modes in which it is used, and the method of adapting it to the ever varying wants of individual habitations.

A ventilating flue acting by the aid of heat is preferred to any mechanical power, steam jet, or other apparatus producing the movement of air, as it is simple in its construction, sure in action, not liable to get out of order, economical in its application, and capable of being as easily understood and managed as any ordinary fire-place and chimney flue.

Let it be remembered that the object is not to supersede the use of doors and windows, wherever it is desirable or necessary to resort to them, but to act as an auxiliary under circumstances where they cannot afford the comfort required; to control and remove special accumulations of bad air that may affect injuriously a whole habitation, or even an extended district comprising many buildings, and to meet those specialities of climate such as occur while the temperature varies from 70° to 110°, particularly if the air be at the same time stagnant, and loaded with moisture.

If a house contain air warmer than the external atmosphere, the colder air tends to enter the house below, and the warm air within to escape above.

If the external air be warmer than the air within, the air within tends to escape below like water from any vessel with apertures in it, the warm external air entering above. The movements in this and the preceding case are accelerated or retarded according to the magnitude of the openings or communications between the air within and that without, and the difference in the external and internal temperature.

The principal cause of these movements is the perpetually varying temperature of the air. Air expanding by heat and contracting by cold, the expanded and lighter air can never balance or remain in equilibrio with colder and denser air. The latter, accordingly, sinks under it, if not there already, pressing towards it on every side, and pushing it upwards. Numerous little eddies and rotatory currents accompany the primary movement, which is only part of a larger circle or continuous chain of motions that may be traced from the ascending heated air through the contiguous atmosphere to the descending portion that becomes heated, expanded, and elevated, as long as it is exposed to any source of warmth.

Accordingly, if by any tube, chimney flue, or shaft, as larger and independent chimneys are usually termed, the heated column be secured at all times of a given altitude, it becomes a fixed and definite power that, in ordinary language, draws to it any air, vapor, or gas, permitted to have access by an aperture at the lower part of the chimney.

The current or draught that sets in does not arise from any drawing of the moving air to any point or channel to which it may proceed, though this is implied by the language in common use, but rather to its being pushed by the pressure of the contiguous air no longer balanced by an atmosphere of equal density.

Apertures at the side of the chimney may act in a similar manner if the chimney or flue be not already overloaded with too large apertures below, but they have not the same power as those below, and they may even discharge part of an ascending column instead of drawing in air, if the moving power from the heat exceed that of the upper part of the flue to discharge the air that reaches it.

In the simplest form of application to an individual apartment, it may consist of a tube or flue opening immediately under the ceiling, and formed as near as possible to the ordinary fire flue, receiving warmth from it when in use, and capable of being heated by it at any time, or by some other substitute. Such a flue, if only a few inches square, will have a very powerful effect in removing the vitiated air from the ceiling of any ordinary room, but it will be better if never made less than eight or nine inches square, so as to give at all times a clear area of large dimensions. These flues ought to be lined with a thick coating of tenacious and very porous plaster or pargetting, otherwise, lamps with oils or gas producing much watery vapor during combustion, become objectionable from the deposition of condensed moisture.

The flue explained, however useful in numerous instances, is not to be considered the most desirable adjustment, either in an old or a new building. On any floor, but best of all in the basement or kitchen floor, a brick flue should be commenced in all new houses, and carried to the top of the building. No lateral aperture is made in this flue above the fire-grate, except one for fuel, which is placed as low down as circumstances may permit, and about the same level as the kitchen fire-place, so as to admit of being easily fed with fuel. The air plays freely around and through the fires, according to the amount admitted, and is supplied by a series of channels communicating with the rooms or spaces on which it is intended that it should act. Valves regulate the amount of power placed on the apartments, or other areas connected with it, and thus its action can be directed on any of them individually, or distributed over all.

When a special flue is introduced in a new building, it is desirable to give it power over the following rooms or spaces, viz. the kitchen, scullery, wash-house, closets, cellars, and drains (when they are imperfectly formed, or temporarily opened), the dining-room, drawing-room, bed-rooms, stairs and passages, and other places, according to the peculiarities of individual habitations.

It will be obvious that such communications may be extended or reduced at pleasure. In an ordinary habitation these give sufficient power to meet all the principal desiderata.

Further, when doors and windows are closed this shaft causes cold air to ascend from any place where it may be preferred, entering the staircases and passages generally, or any individual apartment, according to the channels provided for this purpose.

Great attention must be paid to the construction of the fire-place, so that while it shall thoroughly heat the air in the flues, the free space around it shall permit a channel for the passing air fully equal to the area of the flue. The valves must be capable of being open or shut to any extent desirable, in order that its action may be concentrated principally on one or two apartments, where numbers may have assembled.

The size of the flues may be made as various as the requirements of individual habitations demand. One foot area should in general be the minimum for such a flue, even if it be intended only to control the vitiated air from the kitchen, closets, drains, and wash-houses, and apply it occasionally to other places. But if the construction of the house admits it—and there are few places where, with a little management, this cannot be effected—an area twice or even four times as large will be found advantageous by those who prefer ample ventilation. If it be required to sustain a continued ventilation of all the apartments of any house by the operation of a shaft, an area of three or four feet will be desirable in an ordinary house with ten to sixteen rooms.

The amount of special ventilation required in any house is as various as the taste and constitution of those occupying it, the temperature of the air, its hygrometric condition, the climate, the numbers present, the system of lighting adopted, the quality of furniture, and the purity of the air supplied. The perpetual change of season adds a never ceasing variety to the wants of the living frame, the power of ventilating flues, and the emanations which they are required to control. The great point accordingly is to construct such flues and communications as are most imperatively wanted, and to secure the means of enabling them to act generally or locally as may be necessary.

Let it be remembered, however, that a ventilating shaft may be made to act in a much more effective manner than a perpetual fan or punkah in hot weather. These merely move the air in direct contact with the surface of the body without preventing its return, but the shaft discharges utterly and entirely the air that has once been loaded with exhalations from the human system, and increases practically the cooling

effect of any atmosphere, if it be at all below the temperature
of the body, by multiplying the quantities brought in contact
with it in a given time. Pneumatic instruments, as a rotatory fanner, or an air pump, may be used as a power in the
same manner as a shaft, if properly adjusted and sustained
continuously in action.

If a case should occur where it is necessary or convenient,
from special causes, that a flue should discharge smoke or
invisible products of combustion at a lower level than the fire
itself, this may be effected frequently by merely turning the
flue to the course required, after it shall have ascended sufficiently high to have lost the sharpness of the heat it at first
acquires. Such an arrangement is often a great convenience
in removing gaseous products, as they may then be conveyed
from a site where they might interfere with the free use of an
open roof, or the quality of air taken in near it. These products may be dissipated below, or absorbed in the general
action of some greater ventilating flue discharging its products
at an unobjectionable position.

If a flue be merely made to ascend directly from the source
or sources of vitiated air, there is no security in its acting with
the efficiency obtained by the aid of heat. When, however,
the temperature of the external atmosphere is low, and that of
the air discharged considerably higher, it may operate well.
It is proper, therefore, to have the means of communicating
heat above in warm weather, to prevent any danger of the
current being reversed, and then its action may be secured,
though it will not, under parallel circumstances, have the same
power as a longer shaft. Wherever flues are used, the supply
of air to the apartment to be ventilated must meet with no
obstruction, otherwise the vitiated air cannot have any proper

opportunity of escaping. By interrupting or diminishing the
source of supply, the amount of external pressure that produces the ventilating current may be altogether intercepted or
proportionally reduced. The examples are innumerable where,
from inadequate attention to this point, ventilation is often very
imperfectly sustained. Many never stop to realize the fact that
no air will continue to pass out of a building, under any ordinary circumstances, unless a proportional quantity be permitted
to enter.

In the great majority of habitations, the amount of supply of
air is generally insufficient without the aid of doors and windows, and how many are there that have no other source of
fresh air, except what these may afford, or cracks, fissures and
imperfect fittings, and cold chimney flues neither in actual use,
nor warmed by contiguous flues, the ordinary course of the
current being reversed?

It may be laid down, accordingly, that the provision of an
aperture, capable of supplying the largest amount of air which
it may be desirable to introduce from a sheltered source during
the highest intensity of summer's heat, is one of the most
important improvements that can be introduced in a house not
already provided with it. It can be opened or shut at all
times to any extent, without being dependent on any ordinary
doors or windows.

In old houses, any special door or window may be adapted
for this purpose, that can be appropriated to it, if the air
channel proceeding from it can be led directly into the passage or staircase, and connected with such provisions as may
be used for general or local warmth.

In building a new house, the construction of a general supply
should attract very special attention, and any possible sources

of vitiated air be carefully avoided. It will also be very desirable in many localities, to bring down the air from some altitude above the ground. This is particularly important where some of the rooms may be likely to be crowded from time to time with large parties or assemblies for business or recreation ; and still more so, if the intended building is to be erected where the ground is apt to be damp, and a moist atmosphere to rest above it, not subject to the free play of atmospheric currents. Even at a height of ten or twenty feet above the ground, the air is of much better quality, in some districts, especially at night. In others it should be taken from the highest available altitudes where it is not exposed to the heat of the sun ; or in danger of being contaminated by the escape of smoke from contiguous chimneys. Fig. 79 indicates a supply of air by a shaft constructed in this manner, which can be reduced in temperature on special occasions by water permit‑ted to descend as a shower, or by the use of ice, when the condition of the air does not render the moisture objectionable, that is thus communicated.

This general supply of air distributes itself in the passages and stairs so as to communicate freely from them with the whole of the house.

A portion of the channel by which it is conveyed can be formed so that all or any part of the air can be warmed or cooled.

The right condition and movement of air in stairs and passages often contributes more to health in individual habitations than any other circumstances. Many are the houses in which a comparatively uniform climate is thus formed within doors, and a free communication sustained by open doors, or open apertures such as internal windows, with all the individual

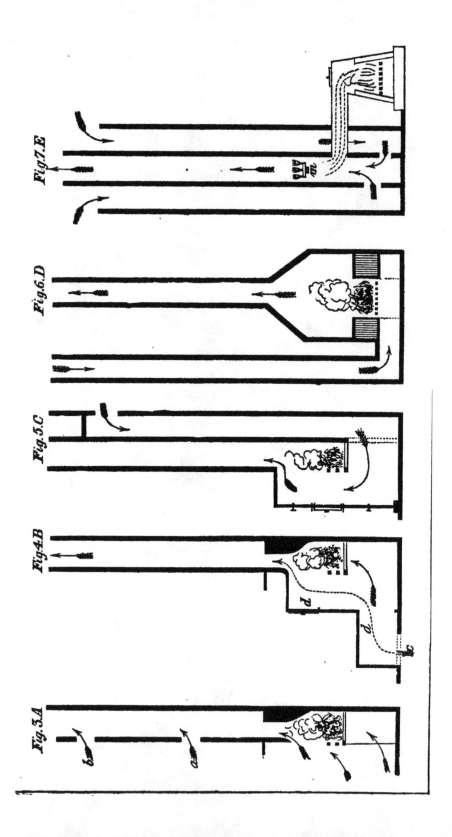

apartments in actual use, through the medium of the stairs and passages.

When the house is not required for crowded gatherings, or overloaded with inmates, and the stairs and passages not over narrow, a window or other opening near the top may be arranged for the general supply of air, descending, then ascending again, and ultimately escaping above; after supplying the individual apartments.

In some houses, louvre doors made with panels constructed in the same manner as the blinds in common use outside of windows, or of porous wire gauze or other textures equally open, have been used on all occasions when they were crowded with company. In other cases the doors are entirely removed, or formed so as to slide into the wall. If the warm air be permitted to escape by a central framework made of perforated zinc from the upper part of any staircase, while the fresh air enters on every side around this central portion, the temperature lost and gained by the escaping and entering air, prepares it sufficiently in many conditions of the external atmosphere.

DIAGRAMS OF SPECIAL VENTILATING FLUES OR SHAFTS.

In examining the importance of introducing a special ventilating flue capable of acting on one or more rooms in every habitation, it will be well in the first place to look to the following details.

If an aperture be made in any chimney flue where the air is heated by a common fire, as a in the flue A Fig. 3, air in general will be drawn in as represented by the arrow. A second aperture may often be made at b with a similar effect, but when these apertures are increased beyond the power of

the chimney, they become inoperative, or a reverse current
ensues.   They are not always to be depended on in sustaining
a ventilating current, so that valves are used to arrest the
return of air or smoke from the common chimney, in using an
aperture above.   If the chimney be made air-tight at the fire-
place, as in the flue B Fig. 4, and a sheet iron tube *d d* be
extended from it to the ceiling of a lower room *c*, then
ventilated air from that lower room may be removed, the fire
acting as a ventilating power upon it.   If there be two
contiguous spare flues in any house, one may be used as
shown in C, Fig. 5, being converted into a special ventilating shaft, and the fire-place receiving no supply of air
except from the other flue.   Any room, passage, closet, or
cellar, may be ventilated by it, forming an air-tight communication between it and the place to be so ventilated, to
which the external air must have access.   Or all of them may
be connected with it, and receive a proportionate ventilating
power by valves regulating the amount of discharge from
each compartment.

In any apartment the fire-place may be converted into a
temporary ventilating shaft acting on any part of the room in
which it may be placed, by rendering the front of the fire-
place air-tight, as in Figs. 4 and 5, and connecting the lower
part with a tube proceeding in the direction required.   In
Fig. 6, D, the flue is withdrawing air from the ceiling of the
room in which it is used.

In cottages or other places containing a single chimney
heated by the smoke from a stove or a central gas lamp,
placed within the flue, as at *m*, a ventilating power may be
induced on every side in the manner shown by Fig. 7, E, and
currents led from any contiguous rooms.

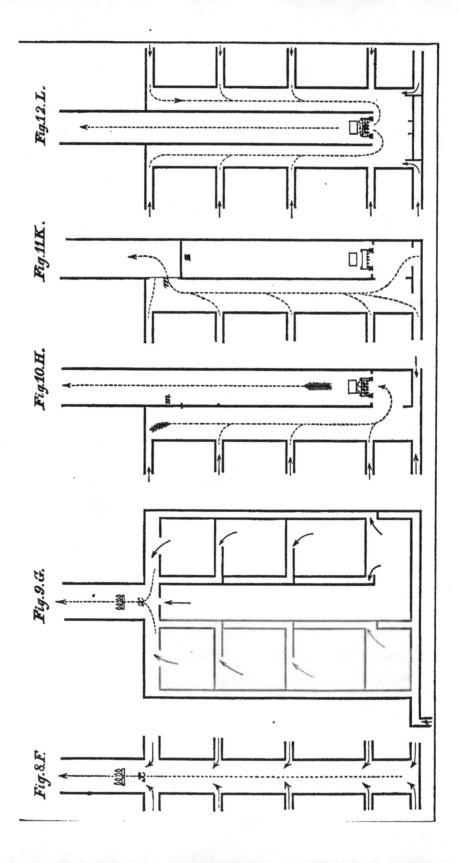

Fig.12.L.

Fig.11K.

Fig.10.H.

Fig.9.G.

Fig.8.F.

If a ventilating turret be erected on the roof of a house, Fig. 8, F, and a staircase or any other descending channel *x* that may be rendered sufficiently air-tight, be connected with it, then, as in the case E, minor ventilating tubes discharging vitiated air can be led into it, and a series of gas lights kindled above at *x*, when the vitiated air is not sufficiently warm without them, to give the requisite ventilating power.

Fig. 9, G, indicates a similar arrangement; a chamber in the roof receiving the vitiated air from minor channels, which communicate with all the places to be ventilated.

The ventilating turrets F and G having no great amount of heating power, in cases where the utmost effect of a ventilating shaft is necessary and when a turret on the roof would not give the necessary heat or altitude, it is requisite to make a descending shaft for collecting and carrying downwards all the vitiated air, and an ascending shaft for giving the moving and discharging power. H, Fig. 10, points out the usual and most convenient form given to such shafts, the arrow indicating the course of the vitiated air. There is no limit to their size, nor to the number of apartments upon which a single shaft of this kind can be brought to bear, the amount of fuel used being proportionate to the ventilating effect required. The higher the chimney, the greater is the power exerted.

In climates where there are great extremes of temperature, the ventilating shaft is often so constructed as to be used in winter without a fire, the temperature of the apartments ventilated when the external air is cold giving the necessary power. Fig. 11, K, shows a shaft similar to H, Fig. 10, provided with a valve opening at *m*, and permitting vitiated air to escape without any previous descent. By changing the position of the valve, *m* is closed, and an opening again restored at *z*, when fire can be employed to give the requisite ventilating power in warmer weather.

In many cases two descending shafts may be formed as in Fig. 12, L, or they may be multiplied to any extent provided the aggregate power required to put as many as are wanted in effective operation at a given time shall not exceed that of the ventilating shaft.

In ordinary habitations a single flue of the usual size will be found very useful, but it is presumed that the time will arrive when no houses containing from ten to twenty rooms will be constructed without a ventilating turret, tower, or shaft from three to six feet square, according to the numbers it may be intended from time to time to invite, and the dimensions of the principal apartments.

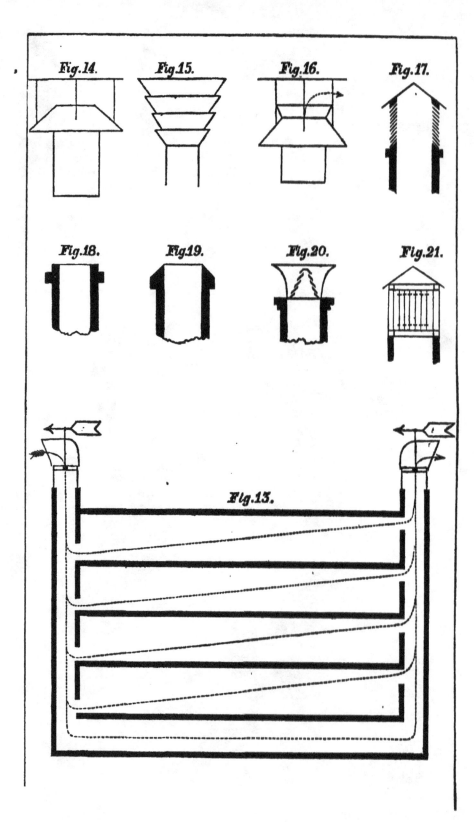

Fig. 14. Fig. 15. Fig. 16. Fig. 17.

Fig. 18. Fig. 19. Fig. 20. Fig. 21.

Fig. 13.

CHAPTER V.

EXTERNAL INGRESS AND EGRESS OF AIR.

In finishing the external aperture of any ventilating shaft or flue, it is of no small importance that it should be well protected from wind and rain, according to the peculiarities of each individual case, and the general intensity of the currents that may prevail in the district in which it is placed. An endless variety of devices have been contrived for this purpose, and few countries have not some form of discharge or protection that has been tested for generations. Till modern times, however, they have not been the subject of much specific investigation.

It is often forgotten that mere apertures of supply and discharge have no moving power that is not dependent on the wind, and that they are accordingly entirely inoperative in calm weather, except in so far as temperature or other causes may influence their action. Hence the necessity of artificial heat, or mechanical power, whenever a specific effect is required, whatever may be the state of the weather. Changes of temperature often promote reverse currents. But when a current of air more or less powerful strikes upon the top of any flue or ventilating aperture, it will be obvious that the manner in which it impinges may facilitate or retard the escape of air from within, and that one mode may be well adapted to promote the ingress of fresh air, and another to facilitate the discharge of vitiated air. The union of both produces the

highest ventilating effect, as in Fig. 13, where a lateral ventilation is given by the entering current, while it is assisted by
the action of the external air on the discharge aperture on the
other side.

The form of discharge, Fig. 14, used so much in some parts of
the United States, and which is especially recommended by Mr.
Emerson, is more simple and not so liable to injury. The corresponding arrangement for the supply of air is seen in Fig. 15.

A paper placed in the author's hands by Professor Horsford,
of Cambridge, Mass., contains much valuable information on
this subject, being the result of a series of experiments of a
Committee of the Academy of Science, in Boston, in which he
was associated with Dr. Wyman, Prof. Pierce, and Prof.
Lovering. Fig. 16 points out the form of cap to which they
have given the preference. It is more powerful in its action,
though not quite so simple in its form. The louvre turret,
Fig. 17, is much used in many external finishings, whatever
additional provisions may or may not be made within it.
Reversing the position of the louvres promotes an internal
current. In numerous buildings the projection of some bricks
near the top forms the only assistance given to the flues in the
discharge of vitiated air, Fig. 18. In large shafts or chimneys
having no cap or protection above, the upper portion, Fig. 19,
is usually inclined at an angle of 45°. Fig. 20 indicates a form
of protection that was found extremely useful in a site where
a flue was subjected to strong and sudden lateral currents from
an irregular surface in its vicinity.

In many places a few iron rails placed perpendicularly
around the top of a chimney, or crossing each other at various
angles, will often extinguish the action of local currents tend-
ing to produce down-draughts in fire or ventilating flues.

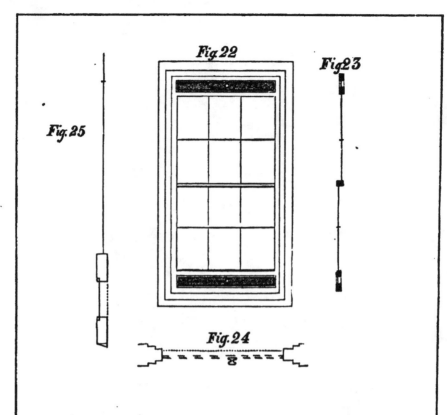

Fig. 25

Fig. 22

Fig 23

Fig. 24

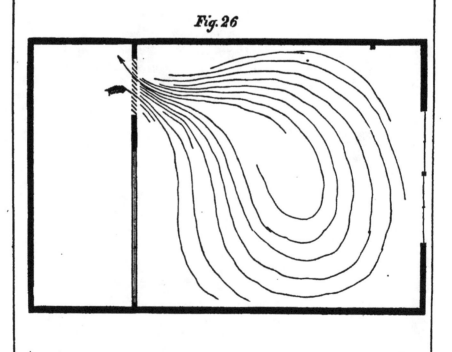

Fig. 26

CHAPTER VI.

THE WINDOW.—INTERNAL WINDOWS.

In an apartment with one window, where air cannot be obtained of an agreeable quality from the passages, and where the ventilation is in other respects satisfactory, the complaint is that the currents are too strong, when the amount of supply by the window is sufficient.

The object in this case being the reduction of the force of the current, it will often be sufficient to place a porous curtain in the interior which shall spread any air entering from the window over a larger surface, and reduce the velocity as well as extend the area of its movement.

Many arrangements have been made of late years to diminish the force of the entering air at windows, and to permit a variable but limited ventilation to ensue. Perforated glass, glass louvres in a single pane, or panes of perforated metal, have been much in use. They have each a limited effect, according to the extent to which they are used. They are generally too local in their action, and not sufficiently under control.

Where a more careful arrangement is necessary, and where the mere opening or shutting of the windows with a gauze curtain is not sufficient to control the current, the window may be filled up in new houses as indicated in Fig. 22 and 23.

Above and below the ordinary glazing a frame extending the

whole breadth of the windows is formed, and admitting, where it is finished, of a slip of perforated zinc being inserted. It may be left open entirely in summer, and opened or closed to any extent in winter. It interferes in no way with the ordinary use of the window, but is a reserve by which a limited portion of air in a very divided stream may be admitted or discharged above or below.

The upper portion serves as a discharge for air, and the lower portion for the ingress of air, when the ordinary course of currents is not reversed by an excessively high temperature.

Valves of various forms may be added, as in Fig. 24, where the plan shows the valve partially open. Fig. 25, shows an enlarged view of the perforated zinc, with the valve before it closed.

In winter such arrangements temper the flow of air where windows must be used. In summer they permit a limited ventilation, while they exclude insects. For a temporary purpose in moderate or warm weather, a gauze net is occasionally fixed externally, or internally, and the windows freely thrown open when a large supply of air is desired.

THE INTERNAL WINDOW.

Above the doors and below the ceiling, of individual apartments, there is usually a considerable space not applied to any special purpose. If that be opened freely and supplied with a louvre, it may be used as an internal window, enabling each room to draw upon the adjoining passage as a milder climate in summer and winter than the external atmosphere. Many apartments are already provided with such openings, but seldom to the extent that is desirable, and principally in the case of bed-rooms. They afford a great additional resource in promoting ventilation, and may be used for the ingress of fresh air, the egress of vitiated air, or for both purposes, as in Fig. 26.

———

For ventilating purposes generally and assisting in the production of a current of supply and discharge with an intervening area comparatively neutral, the ordinary window with a vertical guillotine movement, above and below, has many advantages, particularly in regulating the admission of small quantities of air. Other windows formed in the same manner as doors, may give a large opening in moderate weather when they are entirely thown back, but they are not so useful during the extremities of severe heat and cold.

With all the resources mentioned, the window, invaluable as it may be, can never render a good ventilating power unnecessary. If it be recollected how often there are times and seasons when the smallest aperture gives a sufficient ventilation, and others when the system is uncomfortable whether it be thrown open entirely or partially, the importance of independent ventilation will be more readily admitted.

It must not be overlooked, however, that even where a considerable amount of diffusion is given, it may not be practicable to prevent the current from a window feeling cold, unless with a very unusually protective dress, and then a warming apparatus must be introduced there, or the air as it enters, be conveyed by tubes or otherwise to a different place. Even an air-tight window, when any one may be confined to a fixed position near it for a long time, is apt to induce a local rheumatism, or cold, if double glazing be not introduced.

CHAPTER VII.

VENTILATION BY THE CEILING.

VENTILATION effected by external apertures solely in the roof and ceiling succeeds well generally, if there be a proper opportunity for the distribution of currents, except when the external temperature exceeds that within, and special provision is not made to meet this case. The entering air can be diffused over the ceiling, or permitted to descend in any manner preferred, as in the case of doors, windows, or other apertures. With very lofty rooms, the descent and ascent do not proceed so satisfactorily.

The use of the ceiling might be very advantageously extended in many cases of ventilation, where it can not only be used for diffusing air, but also be made a medium for returning part of the heat of the escaping vitiated air, without contaminating the entering fresh air. When a single aperture is made in the ceiling of any apartment, the air moves for the most part, if no other escape be provided. as indicated in the internal window, Fig. 26. When there are two apertures in the ceiling, the tendency is to move as in Fig. 27

In many individual apartments, or other places where there is much annoyance from a local draught to a fire or stove, the chilling effect on one side being as objectionable as the heat on the other, the evil may be removed or greatly palliated by

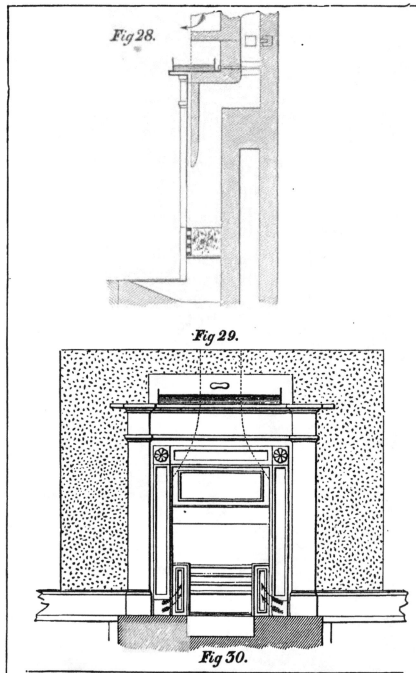

Fig 28.

Fig 29.

Fig 30.

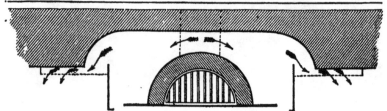

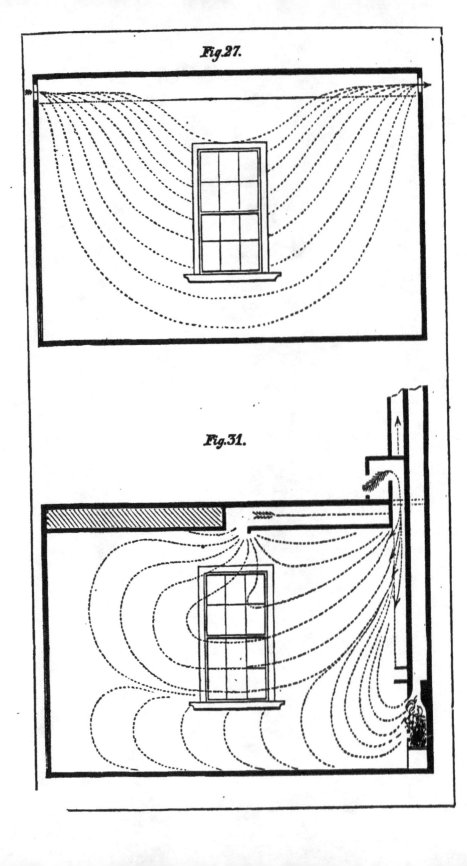

Fig.27.

Fig.31.

similar measures for diffusion more or less completely introduced, as local circumstances may render necessary. And where numbers do not render the air impure by respiration, nor gas lamps contaminate it, this supply may often be given either at the ceiling, wall, or floor, in the vicinity of the fire or stove.

Ventilation by the ceiling, the supply and discharge being both arranged there, is principally valuable in small and low rooms where neither an ingress nor egress for air can be so satisfactorily obtained in any other manner. It is also important in all cases where the escaping vitiated air has to impart a portion of its warmth to the entering cold air.

In large rooms not at all crowded, the ingress requires little diffusion if placed where the current does not fall offensively on any of the occupants.

In small rooms, instead of a few feet of surface being devoted to diffusion, the whole ceiling is sometimes appropriated to this purpose.

When the external air is very warm, the roof should be cooled with water, an artificial current induced by heat, or an internal window or other opening made above the door to facilitate the circulation of air.

CHAPTER VIII.

SUPPLY OF AIR AT AND IMMEDIATELY ABOVE THE FIRE-PLACE.

AN ordinary fire-place is the subject of much complaint by
an invalid, who is exceedingly sensitive to any cold currents
of air.

On examination it is found that the chimney flue is many
times larger than is required for the grate. Contracting it,
accordingly, at the top, the evil is in a great measure
removed.

A further reduction in the current may be produced by
supplying the room with air as shown by Figs. 28, 29, and 30.
These indicate a supply of fresh air introduced behind the
grate, where it is warmed previous to gaining access to the
apartment, and its distribution at b, c, d, and e. The larger
the proportion of fresh air admitted near the fire, the less is
there to traverse the room before it is warmed, and produce a
disagreeable draught.

In small rooms or offices constructed subsequent to the
erection of the building to which they are attached, air is
often advantageously introduced in this manner at the
chimney breast alone, Fig. 31, or at the ceiling, the whole
surface being made porous by gauze steeped in a solution to
render it less inflammable if perforated zinc be not used.

Many buildings are provided with an excellent heating
apparatus, but when this is not combined with such sys-

tematic ventilation as the peculiarities of the circumstances require, it often acts at a great disadvantage, being ill supplied with fresh air, and unable, consequently, to give the equal and genial temperature it might otherwise produce.

It cannot be too carefully remembered that ventilation has always a cooling effect, except when the temperature of the air entering the apartment to be ventilated exceeds that of the living frame. The greater the amount of ventilation, accordingly, the greater the amount of heat required in cold weather to render it agreeable. Further, the more gentle and the more general the approach of the air, the less the elevation of temperature necessary. And lastly, the less the interference of any local cooling power, as cold window glass, the greater the perfection of the general result.

Double windows are perhaps less frequently used in the United States than in any other countries exposed to parallel extremes of heat and cold where they have similar facilities for obtaining glass. Their use would be very desirable in many places, and save much fuel in winter. In some apartments the introduction of double windows would be equally advantageous in summer and winter, where air is supplied and discharged by other arrangements.

CHAPTER IX.

PREVENTION OF THE RAPID ESCAPE OF FRESH WARM AIR.

A ROOM supplied with air from a heater is found to discharge the air that is conveyed to it too rapidly, unless an aperture connected with the ventilating flue on a level with the floor be opened instead of that at the ceiling. But when this is done, the air is not so fresh as is desired. What remedy should be adopted?

Let more air be supplied at a less elevated temperature by a wider channel. If this mode cannot conveniently be carried into effect, let the entering air be conveyed to a channel formed on as many sides of the apartment as may be accessible, and let it be bridled at its escape from this channel by perforated zinc, or some other substitute, that permits a limited portion only to escape at any individual place.

Fig. 32 indicates a hot ascending current escaping rapidly when the upper ventilating aperture alone is open, the vitiated air remaining in a great measure below.

Fig. 33 exhibits the course of the air when the lower flue is opened.

Fig. 34 points out the alteration adverted to, and the subsequent progress of the air.

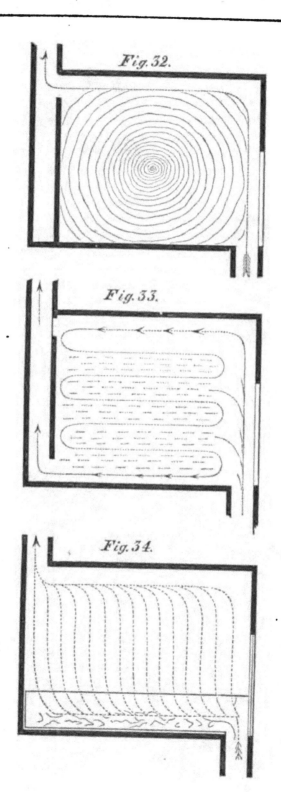

Fig. 32.

Fig. 33.

Fig. 34.

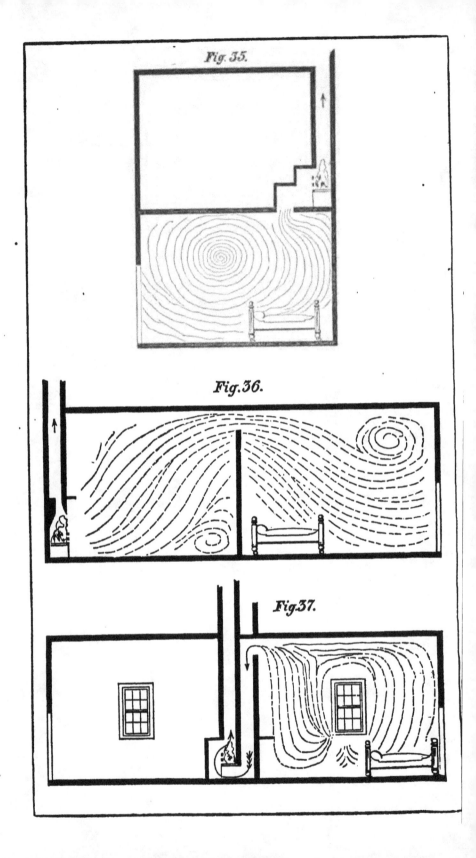

Fig. 35.

Fig. 36.

Fig. 37.

CHAPTER X.

VENTILATION OF BED-ROOMS IN CASES OF YELLOW FEVER.

A CASE of yellow fever has occurred in a private house; some of the inmates are anxious not to remove if there be any plan by which danger of infection communicated by the atmosphere from the patient can be avoided. They have some apprehensions from this cause, but none from any other source. The relations of the invalid insist on rendering personally every attention in their power. The house has ample accommodation, and several spare rooms, but has no resources for ventilation except some flues for supplying hot air to special apartments. An iron heater gives the required temperature in cold weather. The temperature during the three preceding days has not been below 70° nor above 96° in the shade. The hygrometer has shown an unusual excess of moisture.

If the following course be adopted in respect to the ventilation, all the vitiated air in the patient's room will be entirely prevented from entering any other part of the house, and therefore, from the cause specified, no danger need be apprehended; nor is there anything to prevent many other sources of infectious effluvia being controlled in a similar manner.

Fig. 35 indicates an upper room, immediately above the patient's room, with its fire-place arranged to act in the manner explained under "Shafts" and "Special Flues," and supplied solely from the patient's room, the fresh air being drawn to it from the passage or any contiguous apartment, the door being rendered porous, and no larger opening allowed at any time than the fire-place above can command.

Fig. 36 points out another method of effecting a similar object, the two apartments in use being on the same floor.

In Fig. 37 a modification of the same arrangements is seen. Every habitation being subject to sickness, these modes of securing ventilation should be familiarly known.

The ventilation, wherever it is desired, may be carried still more fully into operation, and a stream of air made to pass continuously over the body of the patient, every portion of this stream being rapidly removed. The air may be medicated also, so as to become more powerful in its action in any manner the attending physician may prescribe, but this can be effected most satisfactorily in the manner adverted to in the chapter on artificial atmospheres.

With the arrangements explained by the above figures the following results can always be secured :

1. Relief of the patient by the ventilation of the sick chamber.

2. The prevention of any air from it entering any other apartments.

3. The diminution of risk or danger to those who enter the sick chamber, particularly if they never do so when hungry or fasting, as there is then less tendency to absorption from the air.

4. The decomposition of all animal exhalations if the ventilating fire be sufficiently strong, and the consequent removal of apprehension of danger in contiguous habitations.

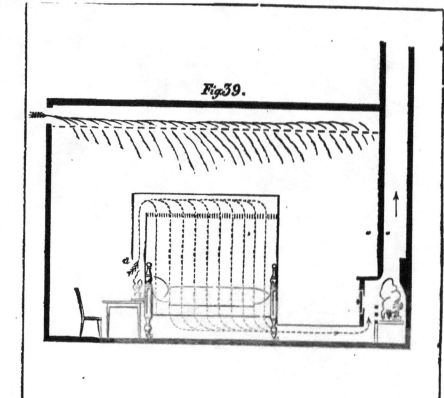

Fig.39.

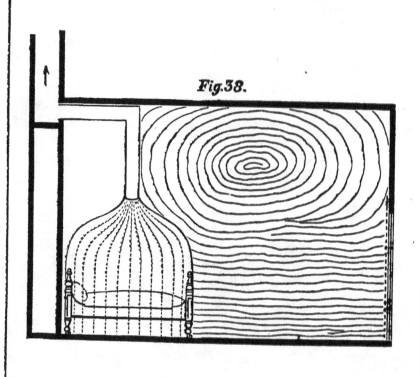

Fig.38.

CHAPTER XI.

VENTILATION THROUGH THE MOSQUITO-NET IN CASES OF SICKNESS AND GREAT IRRITABILITY.

An invalid affected with fever, and in a state of great irritability, is much annoyed with mosquitoes, and when he uses the mosquito-net he either feels, or imagines he feels, an oppressive atmosphere adding to his sufferings. What course should be taken in this instance?

If the mosquitoes cannot be kept out of the apartment in question with such means as are available, and the ordinary net over the bed must accordingly be used, a ventilating tube (Fig. 38) about six inches in diameter should be attached to the upper portion of the net, and connected with any ventilating power that can be made to bear upon it. With a tube of the magnitude mentioned, a small ventilating power such as the common lamp will be sufficient.

There are many constitutions that suffer more annoyance from the mosquito than from all the variations of the atmosphere to which the district they inhabit may render them liable. When there is a calm, and the temperature of the surrounding air nearly coincides with that of the body, every kind of gauze veil or fibre near or around the body diminishes the circulation of air, and hence, great relief is afforded at times by the ventilation indicated, especially if the room be defective in other respects in ventilating power.

CHAPTER XII.

ARTIFICIAL ATMOSPHERE IN THE SICK CHAMBER.

IT is often necessary in the sick room to produce temporary artificial climates, and to submit the patient for a longer or shorter period to the action of a drier or more moist atmosphere than the air of the district presents. In hospitals and other medical establishments special apartments should be constructed for this purpose. The dry and cold air bath and the steam bath indicate suitable means on a small scale. When it is desired to make temporary arrangements for the object mentioned in a private house having no special ventilating power, and where the bed-room is too large for the object in view, curtains may be thrown around the patient's bed from the ceiling to the floor, using porous gauze considerably closer than the mosquito net for diffusing the air used, and giving within these curtains an ascending or descending movement to the air as may be preferred. In Fig. 39 a descending movement is indicated, the diffusing gauze being placed under the roof of the bed. Any ordinary fire-place may be converted into the ventilating power with the use of a few bricks, or some sheet iron, providing apertures for fuel and for regulating the fire.

Where etherial, oleaginous, or other heavy vapors are used in this manner, a descending current is generally preferred, the materials being conveyed to a tube, *a*, immediately above a table where they are converted into vapor, passing by it as the figure indicates.

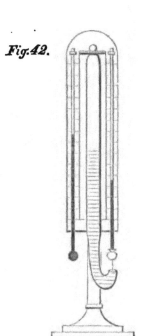

Fig.42.

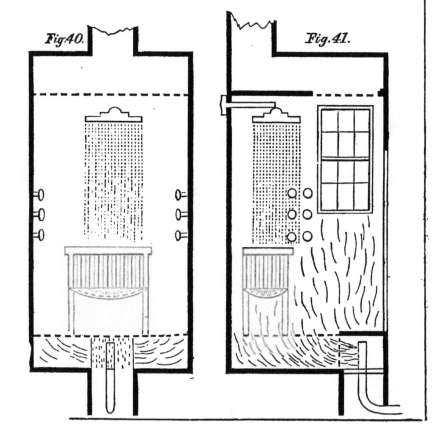

Fig.40.

Fig.41.

CHAPTER XIII.

SMALL CHAMBER FOR ARTIFICIAL ATMOSPHERES.—VENTILATED AIR,
STEAM AND SHOWER BATH.

ARTIFICIAL atmospheres may be formed in apartments on a larger scale than are indicated in the preceding figure, the means
employed being proportionate to the magnitude required,
and the numbers present at a given time. They are prepared
most effectually by transmitting the ingredients necessary into
an air channel through which a regulated current of air is
made to pass. This current may be put in motion by a mechanical power or by a heated flue. The latter is preferred for all
ordinary purposes. For one person, a small chamber lighted
by glazing it on one side and in front, sufficiently large to
admit a chair, and allow any individual to stand erect in it, and
having a platform or floor about four feet square, is sufficient
for common use. An area of two feet six inches by three feet
may be substituted where it is desired to economize space and
materials. In this chamber, supplied with one flue for the
admission and another for the discharge of gases and vapors,
hot air, cold air, moist air, dry air, or any other atmosphere
may be conveniently applied to the system as a means of
preserving health or curing disease.

The accompanying figures, 40, 41, indicate a chamber of
this kind which it is recommended to provide in ordinary
habitations, and also in hotels and lodging-houses where numbers are congregated.

Seated in the chair shown in the figure, each individual can, according to his own taste, subject himself to a powerful current of warm or cold, dry or moist air. Or he can have a shower bath of hot or cold water, or of water at any intermediate temperature.

But the arrangement is prized principally for the combination which it gives of a steam bath, in which this powerful agent can be mixed with warm air in any proportion it may be proper to adopt in producing a sudorific effect, while any admixture of volatile ingredients can be communicated to the passing air, the skin being exposed continuously at the same time, or as frequently as may be desired, to ablution with a warm shower bath. The hands and body are not impeded from the fullest opportunity of using friction cloths. The whole surface of the lungs and skin is subjected in the bath to the free oxidation of the air, and warm and palatable diluents being drunk copiously there to sustain the strength and promote perspiration, a quantity of water passes through the blood in a short time which has the most wholesome and purifying influence. Care must be taken to reduce the circulation of the blood slowly in an adjoining warm room, after leaving this bath, before exposure to the external atmosphere.

The pulls shown on either side of the chair regulate the admission of air, the discharge of vitiated air, the ingress of steam, and the temperature of the water used as a shower bath.

By these varied means, much additional power is given to the steam bath, while the offensive atmosphere attendant on its ordinary use is entirely obviated. Such a steam bath, in its simplest form, should not cost more than a few cents each time it is used, where it is provided for numbers.

CHAPTER XIV.

DRY AND MOIST AIR.

A CONSTANT cough attacks an invalid in frosty weather, while the skin feels harsh and dry, and these effects are increased when a stove in the room he occupies is in use, though an iron basin containing water is placed upon it.

What remedy is available? Let a larger surface of water be exposed to heat with the view of adding more moisture to the air. Let a well tinned or porcellaneous vessel be substituted for the iron vessel containing the water. If the complaints mentioned are not removed, try the effect of boiling water and causing a free discharge of steam into the room, till it begins to condense rapidly like hoar frost on the windows.

Where any source of pure steam is available in the vicinity a small branch pipe from the boiler may be used, for its introduction.

In hotels, lodging houses, or other crowded habitations, where boilers are always available, the steam has often an offensive oily odor. It can then, at all events, be used in heating the porcellaneous or other vessel from which the purer steam can be prepared. In large buildings, where there is the opportunity, moisture conveyed to air by a steam pipe should be mingled with the ventilating current of supply proceeding to any apartment, being then more generally diffused.

4

Where the wet bulb hygrometer is used, Fig. 42, an atmosphere that is so charged with moisture that the ordinary thermometer indicates a temperature about five degrees higher than the thermometer having the bulb covered with muslin, and moistened, is found to be generally acceptable in England. In this country the atmosphere being usually much dryer, or, in other words, having a greater dissolving power, it may be desirable not to give so much moisture as may be required to produce a similar quality of air in this respect. A nearer approximation to it, however, would in all habitations heated with little addition of moisture, produce a great improvement by reducing excessive evaporation from the surface of the lungs as well as from the surface of the body.

If, on the other hand, air be too moist, and the temperature be not high, then nothing corrects this evil so conveniently as the communication of heat. It may not actually remove the moisture, but it gives the air a greater dissolving and retaining power, producing, therefore, an equivalent effect.

It is rarely that measures are resorted to for the actual removal of moisture, in consequence of the expense, except when this is effected by cold, or by the absorbing power of quick-lime, an agent of great value for this purpose in the sick chamber, in rooms that are occupied almost as soon as they are plastered, and in damp cellars.

CHAPTER XV.

EXCESSIVE USE OF GAS IN NUMEROUS HABITATIONS.—MEANS OF VENTILATION NOT PREVIOUSLY INDICATED.

A HOUSE previously comparatively comfortable has been rendered intolerable since the introduction of gas, an excessive brilliancy of illumination being sustained which it is not agreed to reduce.   An improvement in the state of the atmosphere is desired to be effected solely by the ventilation of the gas lamp, or such other measures as shall effect this object with the least additional alterations.

In no city where gas is extensively used are there any causes more productive of vitiated air than gas lights accompanied with inadequate ventilation.

The ordinary course of the products of its combustion is to strike the ceiling and recoil, descending to a greater or less extent according to local currents and eddies, and the level of any aperture by which they may escape.   See Figs. 1 and 2.

Where there is a large consumption of gas, and the products not removed by special provisions, the whole of the atmosphere of the houses, hotels, offices, or stores, is often tainted with them to such an extent that they are palpable to the taste as well as to the nostrils, and marked in their effect upon the inmates, whose pallid countenances and purple lips too often speak an unmistakable language as to its influence upon their systems.   This becomes still more expressive when dyspeptic symptoms begin to indicate still further effects.

The gas stove, so great a convenience in numerous small apartments, stores, and offices, where a more economical source of heat cannot be introduced, or receive the necessary attention, becomes to many a slow poison when not provided with a chimney in the same manner as a common fire-place.

In numerous cases, if the facility of regulation and management be taken into consideration, the absence of dust and the continuity of its action, a small amount of heat may be supplied at less cost with gas than in any other manner, and consequently these inducements to its still more extended use should draw more attention to every improvement that can be introduced in promoting the removal of the products of its combustion by ventilation.

Very simple arrangements permit the heat, as well as the light of gas lamps to be rendered available in many apartments, though the products of its combustion should be withdrawn. The combustion of a small amount of good gas is not more objectionable than the products of respiration.

In London, Paris, and New York, as well as in the great majority of towns, many are the apartments where the winter heat is moderated, not only by the radiation from gas lamps, which is not injurious, except where it acts oppressively on the forehead, but also by the recoil of vitiated air, without which the cold in severe weather would be intolerable, a very inadequate supply of heat, or none, being given by other means.

The accompanying figures show the general arrangements introduced in ventilated lamps for the direct discharge of vitiated air. In others, its escape by the ceiling has already been indicated. The use of ventilated lamps admits of many movements of air in ventilated rooms, which are altogether incompatible with the use of unventilated gas lamps, or the

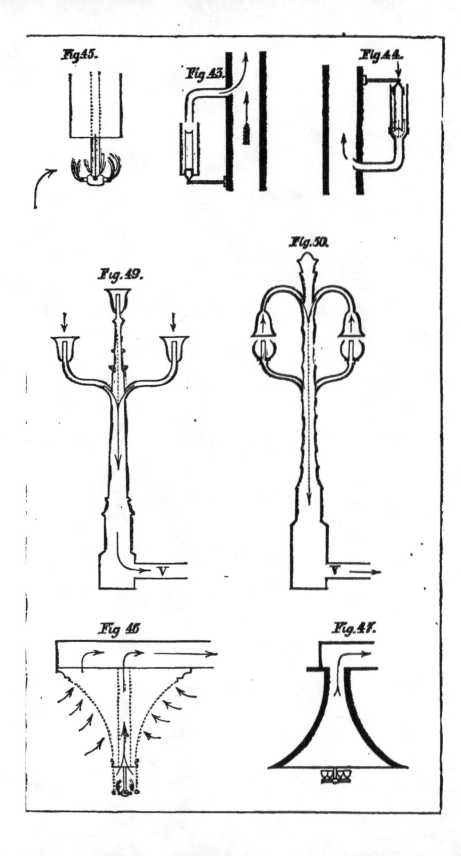

Fig.45.

Fig.43.

Fig.44.

Fig.49.

Fig.50.

Fig 46

Fig.47.

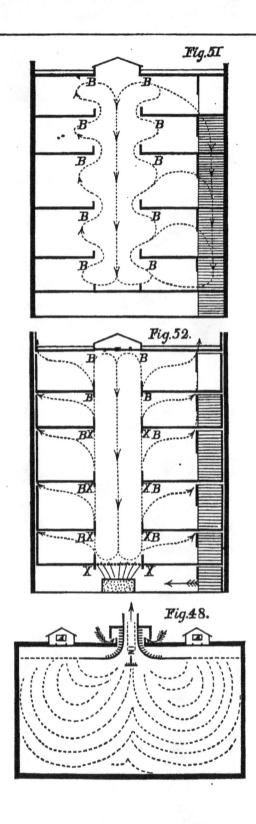

Fig.51

Fig.52.

Fig.48.

excessive use of oil or candles under similar circumstances. Where lamps are placed externally, the light only, and not the products of combustion, being permitted to enter, the same object is attained as by the ventilation of lamps, whether they are arranged outside of windows, or above glass in the ceiling.

Fig. 43 shows an Argand gas-burner, ventilated by a tube led into a chimney flue, the products of combustion mingling with the ascending currents from the fire-place. Where there is a proper opportunity the tube should discharge its products by the shortest course into the external atmosphere. The tube must not then be so long as to permit the external air to cool it to such a degree that moisture from the products of combustion is condensed within it, and returned upon the lamp. In cases where this is not attended to, it is productive of great inconvenience. When the flue into which the products are discharged becomes damp, from a similar deposition in summer, when no fire is used, more air should be permitted to enter by a separate ventilating aperture, and a fire kindled occasionally for a short time to remove condensed moisture and warm the flue.

Fig. 44. Here the current of the argand flame is inverted, the products of combustion being at first drawn downwards. In this, and similar cases, a flue having considerable ventilating power, and always equal and steady in its action, is essential for satisfactory results.

Fig. 45 points out a ventilating tube withdrawing the products of combustion from four fish-tail burners, and modifying the form and appearance of the flames.

Fig. 46 indicates a ring of several burners, ventilated by a similar tube, and the general vitiated atmosphere of the apartment permitted to escape by a perforated metallic frame placed around it.

Fig. 47 shows a very different arrangement where the lamp is placed under a hollow pyramid of a dead white plaster or enamelled porcelain surface; the convex surface distributes the light over the floor with great equality.

Fig. 48 illustrates this form of lamp applied to a room supplied with air from the roof, and warmed as it enters by the outer surface of the gas ventilating tube. In summer air enters at AA. In winter the valve, z, prevents the too rapid escape of the warm products of combustion.

Figs. 49 and 50 indicate pillars for lamps used in special positions either in rooms, halls, or stairs, where it is requisite to lead the products of combustion downwards in a ventilating flue, V, leading to a shaft acting with power on them.

In many stores where manufacturing operations are carried on in the upper rooms, long ranges of gas lamps are fixed on the different floors, as at B in fig. 51. The large opening generally left for light on all the floors where the building is deep, connects them practically into one great room, so far as the atmosphere is considered, and much heat as well as a vitiated atmosphere predominates above, while a large portion of the vitiated air cooled by the external glazing, descends to the lower floors, not the less injurious, though more insidious in its influence, when masked by the lower temperature thus acquired.

Even in many places where no manufacturing operations are carried on, as in some buildings with show rooms above the principal floor, the same deleterious atmosphere may be observed.

The most important object, wherever it is practicable, is to arrange the lamps in such a manner that the waste heat they evolve shall warm the entering fresh air and not contaminate it with the products of combustion. At all events means should be adopted for discharging the principal products of combustion from the ceiling of each individual floor, as pointed out in Fig. 52, adapting details to each particular case. Let there be double glazing in the ceiling where the sky-light is placed, and the individual floors isolated wherever glass can be introduced for this purpose. X indicates a cornice board added at each ceiling to facilitate the discharge of bad air by the flue in the vicinity. A heating apparatus becomes essential in many establishments whenever any ventilation is introduced, if advantage cannot be taken of the heating power of the gas.

A reference to the figures will show that without the cornice-board, x, the stream of the products of combustion from the gas burner must tend, in part at least, to overflow at the edge of the great opening connecting the different floors; but with this board, the warm air spreads more largely under the ceiling till it reaches the open flue, where it escapes.

CHAPTER XVI.

COMPOUND MOVEMENT OF AIR FOR AN ASTHMATIC INVALID.

An asthmatic invalid of an extremely irritable temperament has an office adjoining some houses that are to be pulled down, and replaced by others. He fears, from former experience under similar circumstances, the effect of dust on the air that he breathes, and is desirous that every possible precaution shall be taken to exclude it from his office. Though small it is much frequented, and the door frequently opened to a crowded passage generally loaded with dust when the workmen outside are pulling down houses.

Double doors should be provided in the first instance, and so that one must be shut before the other can be opened. The window should be made absolutely air-tight by painting or pasting it, if necessary, with paper. Let openings be secured for the ingress and egress of a sufficient supply of air, and let it be introduced through a flue or channel where a small stream of water sustains a perpetual artificial shower, Fig. 53, wherever the surrounding atmosphere is loaded with dust. Let the floor be made of an open texture by means of this space, instead of flooring boards, and let the ceiling be porous, a connection being established between the spaces above the ceiling and below the floor. The currents proceed in the manner indicated, the power of the ventilating flue being divided in any required proportion between the ceiling and the floor by the valves a and z.

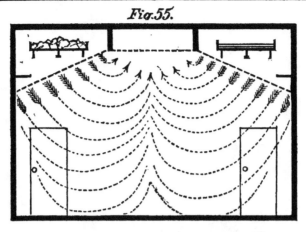

Fig.55.

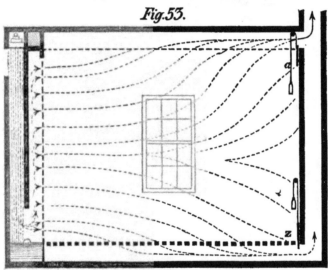

Fig.53.

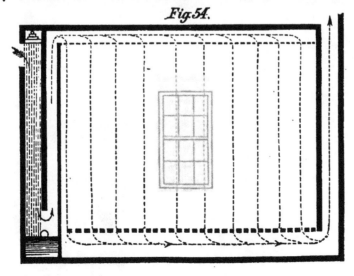

Fig.54.

CHAPTER XVII.

A DESCENDING CURRENT.

If a descending current be alone provided, such as is preferred in some hospitals for special patients, a larger quantity of air is requisite than is desirable according to the preceding arrangement.

The following Fig. 54, indicates the adjustment with a descending current, a ventilated gas lamp being used at night so as to remove all vitiated air from this source.

In very special cases, a stream of air may be introduced in such a quantity that it leaks outwards at every aperture; with bellows, fanners, pumps, or any mechanical power this effect can always be produced where an artificial current is required without the aid of a descending shower, or of a ventilating shaft.

In extremely crowded rooms a pure descending current proceeding from the ceiling to the floor is always objectionable, unless the supply be so ample as to carry the vitiated air in a large stream directly downwards, the products of respiration and exhalation being otherwise apt to linger around the body. A mixed or compound movement, such as is shown in the preceding chapter, is preferable, where no special circumstances render the direct descent important.

CHAPTER XVIII.

COOLING ROOM.

A COLD, or cooling room, provided as a retreat by day or night during the extreme heat of summer, is a valuable addition to any house in some climates, and in many cases of disease forms one of the most important resources in the hands of the physician.

Fig. 55, shows the structure of a powerful cooling room, the air being supplied from chambers above in which any temperature can be given to it by apparatus charged with ice or water. From these it descends gently on either side, vitiated air escaping by a central discharge.

When there is a choice in the position that can be assigned for such a room it is better to place it towards the north, where it may receive the daylight by a double window on the coolest side of the house, the three other sides being entirely under ground when this is practicable, or at least insulated by thick and non-conducting walls from any contiguous offices, cellar, or apparatus, that might otherwise tend to communicate warmth. No air being permitted to enter except by the chambers above or by the doors at the foot of the stairs leading to this room, any special temperature may be communicated to it that may be required, and ventilation sustained, by a channel proceeding from the centre of the ceiling to a ventilating shaft or flue.

The value and luxury of such an apartment is scarcely to be

appreciated by those who have not had the opportunity of testing it in hot and sultry climates. The underground palaces of India, the caves used for the supply of air to some Roman villas in former ages, as well as the fountains, the protected chambers, and the grasses used for the evaporation of water in many warm climates, all suggest that this subject should receive more attention in modern buildings.

Some prefer the daylight to be entirely excluded so as to prevent any accession of heat whatever from external radiation. This may be important in the more extreme cases of high temperature, and where rocks, gravel, or other materials surrounding the walls on every side can exert a continued cooling power upon them. In such a case the walls and floor should be made of thin and conducting materials.

But in numerous places it is important to have such a room capable of being used with daylight. Many individuals can proceed with their ordinary engagements in such an apartment, while restlessness and fatigue attend them in all others, with the higher range of temperature that the external air produces in ordinary rooms. Some invalids, and especially irritable temperaments and children, often regain much strength, and experience great relief from oppression when they occupy a cooling room even for a short time.

In some cases, the movement that can be communicated to the air in the cooling room, and the exclusion of a large amount of external radiation, may be sufficient to relieve the system. For others, it may be necessary, from time to time, to wash the walls with water; they should be built with proper materials for this purpose. Some prepare the ceiling and floor also with this view. Marble, slate, or glazed tiles are all suitable, or any non-porous stone. Zinc and perforated zinc are used for the ceiling. Even when the water is far from being cold, its evaporation from the surfaces of the walls reduces the temperature considerably. If a chamber be made above or contiguous to the cooling chamber, and an extensive evaporating surface be provided there, by porous gauze, or otherwise, a reduction of temperature from twenty to thirty degrees may be effected, according to the hygrometric condition of the air; the drier it is, the greater the amount of evaporation, and the lower the temperature secured.

Where abundance of cold water is available at a proper level, a sufficiently low temperature has been attained by making one or more of the walls of two iron plates, riveted together about an inch apart, and perfectly water-tight, excepting a proper entrance and discharge for the water that is allowed to flow through it. With the use of ice this may be increased to any extent desirable.

It must be remembered that a reduction of temperature by evaporation is not an unmixed gain, as it adds so much moisture to the air that it often becomes objectionable from this cause. The less it is resorted to the better, accordingly, after the air shall have absorbed as much water as it can take up without becoming too moist. It must also be recollected that there are some kinds of water abounding in vegetable matter, or offensive gases, that should not be used for this purpose.

When the temperature is reduced very low, so as to make at once a strong, though grateful impression on entering, none should remain long in it at a time. So long as it is highly grateful, and accompanied by no local disagreeable impression from the cold, it is always beneficial. With a more moderate range of temperature it may be occupied continuously without injury.

It will be obvious that the power of a cooling room may be transferred to the principal channels proceeding from any heating apparatus, when it is not in use, and from this by the action of any shaft or other power, to a central hall or individual apartment in large mansions or hotels. In such buildings the cooling room, when much frequented, should have two doors; one for ingress and another for egress, one door alone being used when not so crowded as to require both. The less the doors are opened the smaller the amount of materials required to maintain a proper reduction of temperature.

In the sick chamber ice should be used with caution. When a sufficient reduction of temperature, or at least an adequate impression of cold can be given by a gentle increase in the velocity of the air or by drawing the air from any passage, cavity, or contiguous apartment previously cooled to a proper temperature, this is the best method of proceeding. The direct action of a lower temperature is sometimes preferred, using it with the greatest care, or a stream of water or shower bath properly regulated.

Where a ventilating flue can be brought into action on any room, in some cases of febrile action a damp sheet thrown around the person will produce a powerful and continuous effect, but it should be discontinued when the oppressive sense of heat has gone, and before any shivering or offensive cold is perceived.

Many are the habitations adorned with every mark of luxury and refinement that have no provision whatever for cooling air, and where a fraction of the sum expanded on one of the many statues or paintings, would fit up a small room entirely with marble, and provide a fountain cooling the walls, ceiling, window, and floor, from time to time, to a refreshing temperature. Numerous are the resources that can be brought to bear in cooling any apartment by chemicals, or by the evaporation of special fluids, when ice is not economical, though they have not hitherto been much used in actual practice.

In the adjustments for cooling rooms, where there are several individuals to be consulted as to the extent to which any cooling power should be put in action, it should never be forgotten that, as in public buildings, extreme constitutions are generally the most clamorous for the atmosphere that is most suitable to their individual wants, so they are the last that should be permitted to regulate the ventilation for the majority, unless where out of deference to age, or infirm health, it is agreed to meet their views.

The obvious rule is that the majority should be more especially consulted, and that others, by diet or clothing, should endeavor, as far as possible, to render the same atmosphere agreeable.

This remark necessarily applies to all differences of opinion, whatever quality of atmosphere may be under consideration.

CHAPTER XIX.

ENTRANCES, STAIRS, AND PASSAGES.

In passing from the consideration of individual rooms to houses, whether in the form of the humblest cottage, or the large and crowded hotel, it may be desirable to offer a few observations on entrances, stairs, and passages. These afford particularly an intermediate climate between that of the external atmosphere and the individual apartments, and nothing appears to be more likely to increase comfort in ordinary dwellings than extending to them more generally than has as yet been done, the means of warming that have been long introduced in particular classes of buildings.

As an open fire is not generally provided for such purposes, except where resources are more ample, in the larger class of habitations, stoves, steam and hot water apparatus become more useful, particularly when it is intended to combine the heating of the entrances and passages with the means requisite for communicating warmth in individual rooms.

Entrances and stair-cases should never be made so large as to admit of any hesitation as to the importance of warming them, and thus giving a milder climate to the whole house in winter. More cases of illness often arise from the draughts and currents in houses having apartments and passages at different temperatures than from exposure to the external air, where the person is generally defended by extra clothing from its influence, and where exercise usually contributes to the power of resisting its bad effects, if the exposure be extreme.

When stoves or heaters are in use the intensity of ·the temperature which many of them attain, however admirably numbers may be constructed, is perhaps the most objectionable feature attending their use, excepting an escape of bad air.

Steam apparatus does not appear to advance so rapidly as the many advantages it presents might lead us to anticipate. Hot water apparatus is most desirable in all places where the levels are suitable, but where it is apt at times to be exposed to sudden frost, it is liable to accident to an extent that appears to restrain its introduction in climates subject to severe winters.

Though ventilation may be sustained without any change of temperature in the air put in motion, still this is so rarely the case that in the great majority of instances it is either caused or accompanied by a change of temperature. Further, as the same atmosphere may, within certain ranges of temperature, be made practically to feel warm, temperate, or cool, according to the velocity with which it is moved, it will be obvious that the questions of heating, cooling, and ventilating, are too intimately associated to admit of being separated to any great extent in actual practice.

Perhaps nothing has ever exceeded in perfection the mild and equal temperature given by the ancients to their hollow floors covered by tiles and mosaic or other pavement; but the structure of these habitations, of which the most interesting records are preserved, neither admitted nor required the ventilation demanded in modern times. The Russian, Prussian, and Swedish porcelain stoves present a great extent of surface and a very mild temperature, and the great tendency in recent years has been to imitate them by water, steam, and other apparatus so constructed and used as to command very mild degrees of heat, generally under 212° though not so low as those at which the porcelain stoves are usually worked, the great surface of the latter making up for any deficiency of intensity.

The drum used in the United States for exhausting the waste heat of stoves and fire-places, and the Arnott stoves in England for economizing the use of fuel, have drawn much attention to this point, while the infinite variety of inventions for the use of bituminous coal, coke, and anthracite, have enabled fire-places and heating apparatus to be improved with a degree of skill and perfection, that has extended continuously since Dr. Franklin, Count Rumford, and Dr. Nott directed their attention to these subjects.

In warming individual houses with a general heating apparatus capable of conveying warm air to individual apartments by special flues, the means are rarely provided of throwing its whole power on the passages and stair-cases to such an extent as is often advantageous, allowing all the house to acquire a more uniform climate by opening the door freely and permitting cold air, when not vitiated, to return to a certain extent by the stairs to the apparatus, instead of drawing in all the air that proceeds to it from the still colder atmosphere without.

This should be effected by large double doors or valves on one or more sides of the apparatus, or immediately above it, capable of allowing so large a stream of air to flow from it when they are open, that it never can reach the high temperature usually attained. These valves or doors cannot be made too large, even if they expose the whole of the apparatus above or on either side, proper materials being selected according to

5

the nature of the apparatus in use, and the highest temperature it can produce in the surrounding air.

In addition to the usual supply of cold air to the heating
apparatus by a specific channel at a low level, it is often very
advantageous to use it only partially, and to admit a portion
of air through a porous perforated zinc panel or other aperture
at a higher level, near or at the ceiling of the stair-case. The
warm air is thus tempered by the entering cold air, and the
force of local draughts at a lower level proportionally reduced.
In those cases when the stair-case is used at the same time as a
means of discharging vitiated air, there is no objection to this
arrangement, if proper facilities are given for the fresh air
entering at one place, and the vitiated air escaping at another,
the amount of movement being carefully regulated by valves.

Numerous are the examples where heated air conveyed in
powerful streams to individual apartments ascends directly to
the ceiling without securing any adequate warmth at a lower
level, and the same remark applies to many passages and stair-
cases. Means should be adopted for retaining it for a time at
least, at the floor, or distributing it largely by metallic plates,
frames, or any other suitable apparatus.

In many of the arrangements made with hot water and steam
apparatus in individual rooms, a similar effect is observed,
though not to the same extent. The greater the length and
breadth of apparatus used, and the more horizontal its position,
the more general the warmth, and the more equal and gentle
the movement of the air induced.

Where there are objections to the horizontal position on a
level with the floor, and space is valuable, steam pipes and
perpendicular cases may be substituted. These have the
advantage of exposing both sides to the air, and when in the

form of steam radiators or steam pipes, can be placed along the lower part of individual rooms in frames so as to harmonize with the general structure, and increase the permanent surface of radiant and conducting power retained near the surface of the floor.

In hotels, offices, and other places where numbers exposed at times to severe cold out of doors desire to warm themselves, the upper part of a stove, hot water, or steam apparatus can be made to form part of the floor of the hall, or of any other apartment devoted to this or other purposes. In a large room constructed at Edinburgh a circular open fire at a very low level, and with a descending flue, gave more satisfaction for this purpose than any other apparatus. It was placed in the centre of the apartment, and allowed each according to his distance to select the temperature and radiation that was most suitable. The floor was made of brick, and always well warmed by the fire.

CHAPTER XX.

THE HEATER.

In a house warmed by a heater, Fig. 56, there is often considerable headache experienced in individual rooms. It is increased when gas is used; the staircase and passages are always cold.

There are no ventilating flues to discharge air from individual rooms; the supply to the passage is small, and the hot air entering these rooms has a temperature from 200° to 250°.

Let flues be provided for the discharge of vitiated air, gathering them together in a chamber in the ceiling, from which a small ventilating turret is raised on the roof, where a gas lamp can be introduced. Pursue the course indicated by Fig. 9.

Fig. 56 shows the heater discharging a small quantity of very warm air. Fig. 57 shows the same heater with the brickwork around it altered to give abundance of air.

Large apertures less in number may be introduced at a, a, a, the details above being adapted to the local peculiarities of each individual case, and the valves or doors carefully constructed so as to intercept effectually the progress of hot air where it is not required.

It is not to be expected that when used in this manner it can transmit a stream of air of the same intensity of heat as formerly to individual rooms; but when the valves to the passage are shut, and the whole power thrown upon the same

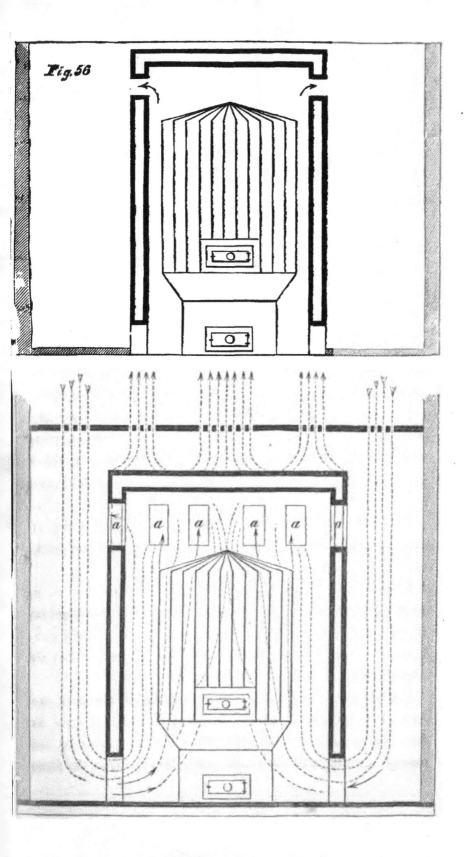

Fig. 56

rooms as formerly, the temperature will not in general be so reduced as to be objectionable, while the general warmth of the house is so very much improved through the medium of the stair-case and passages, that a less elevated temperature than formerly will now produce an equivalent effect. Where the utmost power of a heater at a high temperature is essential to convey the necessary warmth to a distance, it will necessarily be impracticable to make the alteration explained by Fig. 57, and maintain the heat required for the distant room without an addition to the stove.

CHAPTER XXI.

STEAM APPARATUS.

In considering the various modes resorted to for the use of steam in cold weather, wherever the quality of the vapor is good and free from all offensive odor, a large amount may always be thrown directly into the current of cold air as it enters the lower ventilating chambers, taking care not to add more than is rapidly or at least thoroughly dissolved before it reaches the apartments to be ventilated. Arrangements for this purpose economize largely the amount of apparatus necessary during the most severe weather in very cold winters, as the dryness of the atmosphere then renders it necessary to add much moisture in proportion to the previous reduction of temperature, and it serves the double purpose of correcting the dryness of the air and of elevating its temperature.

Iron glazed with a porcellaneous surface, or covered with an extremely thin coat of copal varnish, gives a more agreeable atmosphere than plain iron; rusting iron has a disagreeable odor in general, and all apparatus covered with large quantities of thick oils are very objectionable, and retain an offensive smell for a long time. The paint is prone indeed on all occasions to absorb moisture when cold, and discharge it again when heated, taking with it in solution at least as much material as gives it a perceptible and heavy odor.

Again, as to the form of the steam apparatus used, there is

considerable choice. High temperature steam pipes warmed by steam from a high pressure boiler, are not considered desirable for warming air for general use, however desirable for special purposes of art or manufacture.

Iron tubes have for a considerable time been very largely employed, sometimes as the direct source of steam heat, and on other occasions as the means of conveying heat to iron plates that never attain the temperature of 212°.

Iron vases, statues, plates, and iron, in short, thrown into an endless variety of other forms, have also been used for the application of steam heat, whole floors and passages being warmed in this manner, through the intervention of flat boxes or cases filled with steam. The lower and the more general the heating surface in any apartment, the less the heat required to warm it, and the lower the descent of the rotatory movements of air during the progress of ventilation, except where the heat is transmitted very imperfectly to the floor. A given amount of steam or other heat that warms a room comfortably if placed near or on a level with the floor, will not produce this effect if raised to a higher level, unless this room be very specially constructed for radiation. A variety of steam apparatus termed radiators, which appear to have been recently introduced by Mr. Gold, presents very light and movable frames, or steam cases, that have been found very efficient, and are used with a boiler on which much attention has been bestowed, so as to economize fuel and remove apprehensions as to any danger from steam. It is highly spoken of by Professor Silliman, and had evidently given much satisfaction in different cities where the author had seen it used. Nor does there appear to be any limit to the endless variety of improvement in the details of boiler-making, valves, stop-cocks, and hot

water and steam apparatus, on this side of the Atlantic, of
which Mr. Nason of New York has shown me different specimens, any more than on the other.   In the accompanying Fig.
58, showing a steam-boiler S, warming a house, *a a a a* indicates steam pipes used in different forms for the communication of heat; *b*, cases, such as have often been used for steam;
c, the usual position assigned to the steam radiators, more lately
introduced; and *d d*, iron steam tables, such as are used for
special purposes.

Fig. 59 shows the general appearance of one of these radiators, made of two sheets of iron riveted together, and used by
opening a steam cock at one corner below, for the admission of
steam, and another at the opposite corner for the discharge of
air; this forms a very important element in using it, the temperature attained by the case and the amount of surface
brought into play being regulated by the quantity of air discharged.

Figs. 60, 61, and 62 indicate different modes of using flat
iron cases, such as are warmed with steam, when they are required to form part of the surface of a floor, surrounded on
every side with air by elevating them above the floor, or
arranged with an open space under them, where fresh air is
heated as it enters.

As steam apparatus can be obtained of any form and placed
in any position that may be desirable, its use will probably
be more and more extensively introduced wherever simplicity
and economy are important in heating many apartments in the
same building.

Hot water apparatus rivals steam apparatus in all places
where it is not required to place it at any great altitude above
the boiler, the pressure of water upon the pipes increasing the

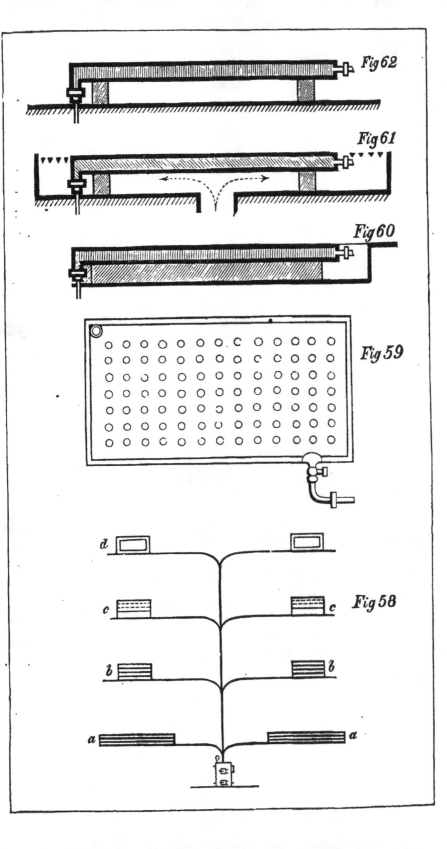

Fig 62

Fig 61

Fig 60

Fig 59

Fig 58

strain upon the joints. It is particularly well adapted for
stair-cases and passages, wherever it can be used on a level
with the boiler, and where there is no risk of sudden exposure
to temperatures sufficient to freeze the water before it can be
warmed.

To the great majority of individuals the open fire is so
pleasing, and allows those previously exposed to cold to acquire
with so much facility the exact amount of heating influence
each may desire, that it is not likely to be superseded in great
entrance halls, waiting rooms, or individual apartments. But
as a means of economy, comfort, and convenience to those
who are long exposed in individual apartments and at fixed
places, other means of general warmth should be introduced,
and the open fire used only in particular rooms, or reduced
largely in its dimensions, wherever many rooms are contained
in a single building.

CHAPTER XXII.

THE LOG HUT.

FIG. 63 indicates a Log Hut of the plainest construction, where in general, and particularly in cold or windy weather, there is too much rather than too little ventilation. The air sweeps through from crevices at the windows, doors, and other places to the large open fire-place. The inmates are subject to attacks of fever at particular periods of the year, when the air within, in unfavorable weather, becomes as oppressive to the invalid as it is offensive and dangerous to the rest of the occupants. The roof transmits great heat in summer weather, and when the fire is used, currents dash in on every side as in Figs. 63 and 65. In winter extreme cold is the principal complaint, and offensive cold currents strike on the back with more and more force in proportion to the strength of the fire.

A ceiling, m, m, Fig. 64, should be formed that will be equally useful in excluding the heat of summer and the cold of winter. At the same time, a partition, p, should be introduced cutting off one third of the hut to be used for a bedroom and for any severe attack of infectious disease. A ventilating flue, f, should be carried from it through the roof, in which a constant current can be maintained by a lamp.

If an adjoining closet, c, be made at the same time, the partition should be so light and movable that it can be taken away with facility.

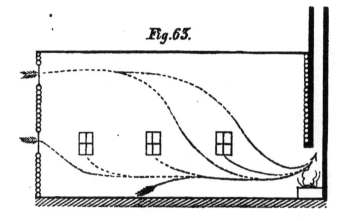

Fig. 63.

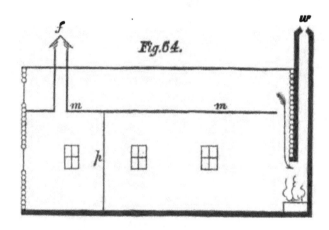

Fig. 64.

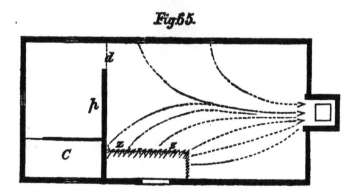

Fig. 65.

The flue should have at least one foot area, and be provided with a valve, and a branch should be led into it from the closet, *c*, above or under the ceiling, according to the mode in which it is made.

At the door, Fig. 65, a screen, *z*, should break the current of supply from this source, and diffuse it as it enters above. At *a*, Fig. 64, admission should be given to a narrow stream of air to intercept currents from doors and windows, and in winter the aperture of the chimney shaft should be reduced at *w*.

In summer the body of the Hut should be so amply supplied with air as to make it incline to press to the sick chamber by the communicating door, *d*, and never from the sick room to the Hut. If the full influence of a cross draught from one window to another should be required in the sick room, the door between it and the other part of the hut should be accurately closed.

By the judicious use of such means, and the careful study of the action of the air-currents within doors, much may often be done to alleviate suffering.

Lime in a caustic state should be used freely in removing refuse, and the utmost attention paid to the cleansing and drainage of surface-water from the vicinity of the hut.

CHAPTER XXIII.

VENTILATION OF A COTTAGE WITH FOUR ROOMS AND ONE CENTRAL FLUE.

THE ventilation of individual cottages and houses, and the desire to introduce improvements that can be rendered available at a moderate expense, attracts a daily increasing attention. In estimating this expense, however, it should not be forgotten that, with ventilation, there is a saving of expense, both in the altitude and area of numerous classes of rooms, that ought to be put down to the credit of the ventilation. Rooms do not require to be built either so large or so lofty for sustaining health when they are provided with the means of systematic ventilation by the action of a heated shaft or any other power. Where dependence is placed on the cubic contents of a room for ventilation rather than on the stream of air passing through it, the supply is in general exceedingly imperfect, unless it be of very large dimensions, and such rooms cannot be constructed except at a great increase of cost.

Apartments are daily constructed for bed-rooms having little more than twice the area of the bed itself, and these can be arranged so as to be better ventilated than others much larger, where this subject does not engage attention. Such substitutes for bed rooms are not advocated for any human beings not on board ship, when better rooms can be obtained, but if it be a

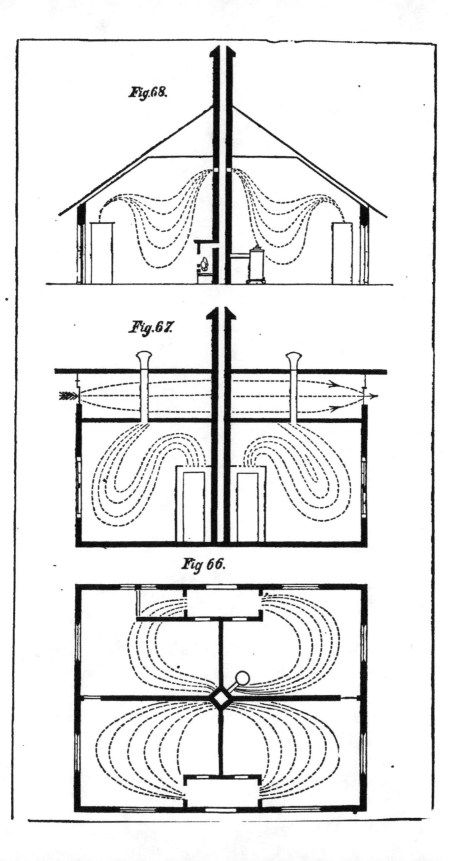

Fig.68.

Fig.67.

Fig 66.

question whether a whole family shall occupy one or two rooms, or make such arrangements as are indicated in the following figures, few, if any, will hesitate as to the many advantages that arise from every effort being made to insure such separate accommodations.

In details the cottage may vary in every individual district according to the materials of construction that are to be obtained, the fuel in use, and the habits, occupations, and wants of those for whom it is provided. Still a supply of air to each apartment from the passage or entrance, and a discharge of vitiated air from the ceiling of each separate space or compartment, or by an internal window communicating with a ventilated passage or entrance, should always be secured.

It is also desirable, particularly in cases of sickness, that there should be one closet at least within the house, whatever other arrangements may be adopted without, and that it should be constructed as explained in another place*, when an abundant supply of water and a proper outlet is not to be obtained.

The cottage, Figs. 66, 67, 68, not being provided with more than one flue and fire-place, though the flue is capable of receiving a stove pipe from any side, the addition of a flue from four or five inches to nine inches square at one of the angles is sometimes useful, where it may be desired to have the power of introducing an extra local fire, or a stove larger than could otherwise be accommodated. In a scullery the flue should be at least nine inches square, and also at any other angle where it may be desired to use it for any particular trade or occupation in which heat or a special stove may be necessary.

In all places the aperture for the discharge of vitiated air

---

* See Drainage.

should be ample, exclusive of the window, where they are used for washing and drying. When the air is damp, during long continued rainy weather, a much larger quantity is required for drying, even though heated, than is usually necessary, and it is important that no moisture should be retained in the atmosphere of the cottage that can be removed by ventilation.

The valves employed in such cottages may be of the simplest description. Slides running in a groove, and capable of being opened or shut with facility by a handle or rod attached to them, or that can be at once applied to them, and move them to the right or to the left, are quite sufficient for ordinary use, and not liable to get out of order. Some prefer a valve with a hinge that admits of being opened and shut like the lid of a trunk.

In winter weather, apertures (or internal windows as they have been called) above the doors of the living room should be freely opened at night, that it may give bed-rooms the benefit of the warm air it may contain, shutting the doors and valves in all unoccupied rooms.

Figs. 66, 67, and 68, a plan and two sections, indicate the cottage with four apartments and one central flue. An open fire-place is provided in one of these only, but stoves can be placed in any of the apartments and connected with it. Two external doors are so constructed as to admit on either side sufficient air for ordinary use. It is diffused at the entrance, and passes from the ceiling of the entrance to the rooms on either side. The vitiated air escapes by vertical tubes discharging into the roof or directly into the external air. Heated air from the roof escapes by the windows shown at both ends in Fig. 67. In winter they are closed.

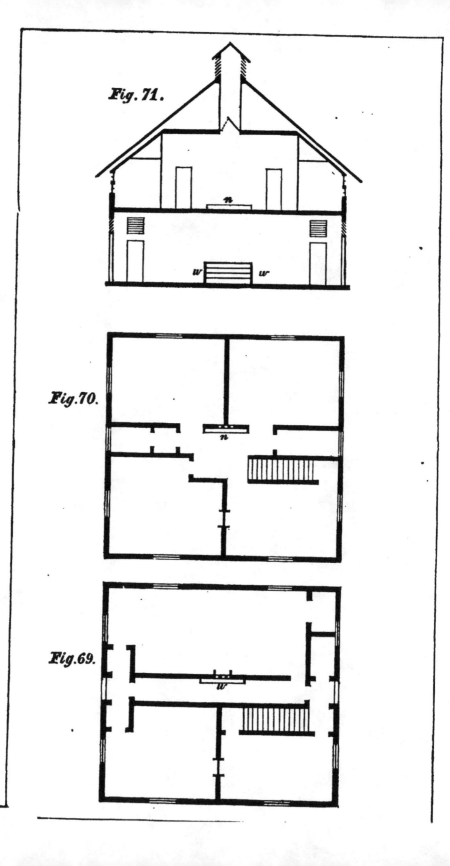

CHAPTER XXIV.

COTTAGE WITH EIGHT ROOMS AND A CENTRAL HOT WATER APPARATUS.

Figs. 69, 70 and 71 show a cottage with an upper floor in which there are four bed-rooms. Stoves can be introduced in the bed-rooms having no fire-places. The roof is constructed in the same manner as in the preceding case. The entrances receive air above the external doors; from them it passes to the contiguous apartments, and by the stairs to the bed-rooms above. Air is also admitted to the upper passages by a window, and is available for all the rooms in the cottage, while it moderates draughts below. The passage is warmed by a mild hot water apparatus, w, and conveys heat to the whole of the cottage. There is also a special provision for removing moist air from linen or other clothes placed above this apparatus in long continued damp weather, the board n, indicated in the upper passage, being then raised so as to admit the damp air to escape directly by the ventilator above.

The principal supply of air is by the apertures above the external doors. Internal windows act as a supply and discharge to individual rooms.

The central flue in the stack of three flues is appropriated to the heating apparatus in the passage. It can be used as a special ventilating flue, and brought to bear on any individual room by connecting it with the third flue, using these two, the second and third, as explained in the description of Fig. 10.

CHAPTER XXV.

VENTILATION OF A LARGER HOUSE.

THIS figure, 72, taken from one of the drawings prepared by the author when engaged on the commission of health for England and Wales, and modified so as to illustrate the use of a heater during a severe American winter, has perhaps been more largely explained, and more frequently the subject of consideration, than any other connected with public buildings. It points out the great objects which it is desirable to arrange in all houses, exclusive of the facilities given by doors, windows, and local fire-places.

An independent supply of fresh air.

A general heating apparatus.

Special flues to and from individual rooms.

The power of heating the staircase, and of permiting rotatory currents there to warm the air generally, with a constant influx of fresh and efflux of vitiated air.

The means of securing or increasing the power of the ventilation at all times by the action of heat in the ventilating turret.

The communication of moisture to the air is secured by the evaporation of water, *w*, from a vessel placed above the heating apparatus, *h*.

The accompanying figure, 73, gives a diagram of the movements of air in the staircase; it is a great object both for econo-

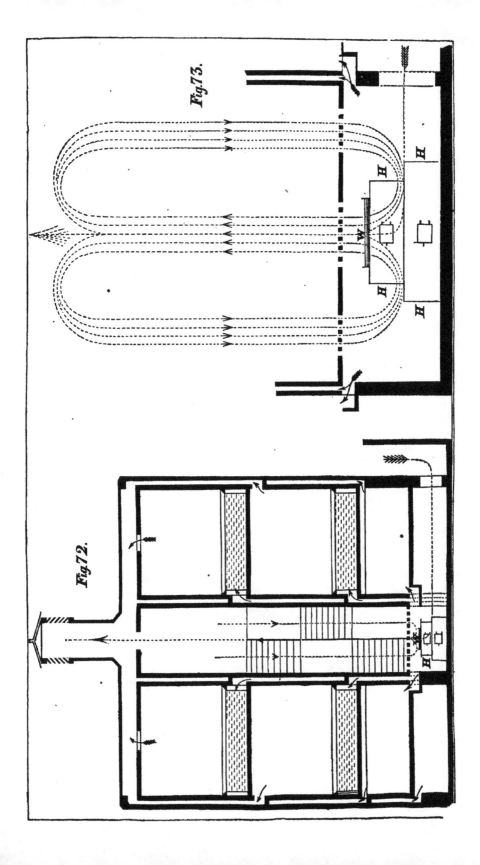

Fig.73.

Fig.72.

my and comfort to heat a large surface of floor at the entrance of houses. This arrests the heat where it is most wanted, and leads to a great but gentle movement of the whole air in the stairs, which is accompanied by local eddies or branch currents to and from individual rooms, according to the temperature, and the extent to which doors, internal windows, or other apertures, permit them to take place.

Wherever there is much furniture, oil paint, a library, or any accumulation of materials that present an extensive surface affecting the freshness of the air, a larger quantity of air ought to be given than is otherwise necessary.

The amount of diffusion of the air as it enters any room is to be regulated by the habits, the clothing, the peculiarities of individual constitutions, the numbers likely to occupy it, and other details altogether local; a small table or screen breaks the impulse of air sufficiently for some constitutions. In others the diffusion that attends its progress from a distant aperture is quite sufficient.

CHAPTER XXVI.

VENTILATION OF A COUNTRY HOUSE.

In the case of the cottage having only one chimney flue every arrangement indicated was laid down in unison with the construction of one fire-place only for ordinary purposes, one apartment being used both for a kitchen and living room, so as to admit of the most limited means being advantageously laid out.

In the present instance, Figs. 74, 75, 76, as in the last, there are more ample resources at command. The distribution and size of the various rooms, and the introduction of a hall, or at least of larger passages and stairs, give greater facilities for the supply of air. The separation of the kitchen forms a still more important feature, and the proper provisions for closets, drainage, and cleansing, give further securities for the uncontaminated supply of fresh air.

In providing a country house where a dining-room and parlor, the requisite number of bed-rooms, and a kitchen, form all the separate apartments desired, and where it is necessary that they should be provided in the most economical manner consistent with good work and comfort, it will be desirable on every other account, as well as for simplifying the ventilating arrangements, that the whole should be contained under one roof, and the apartments placed in the nearest possible proximity to each other.

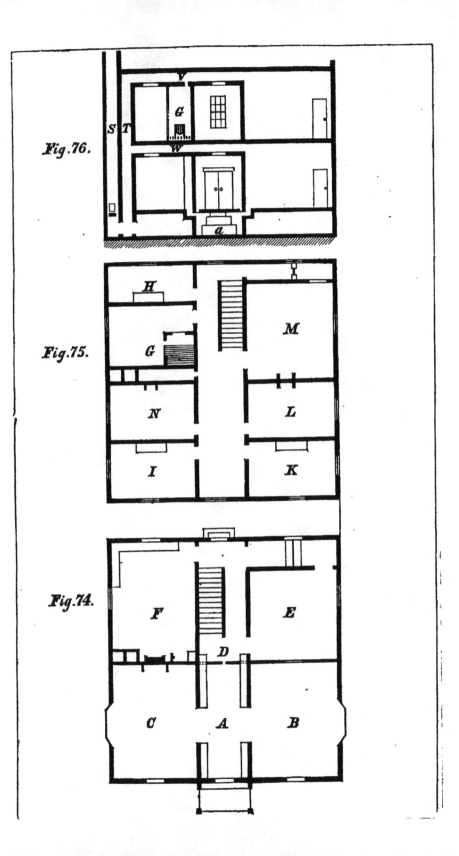

Fig.76.

Fig.75.

Fig.74.

In adopting this course it is not to be supposed that any danger is incurred of injuring the atmosphere of the house generally by drawing in vitiated air from the kitchen and closets. On the contrary, where they are placed under proper control, their tendency is at all times to draw in air from the contiguous passages, and never to discharge any vitiated air they may contain into them.

In this house, the space below the entrance and the principal passage being excavated to the depth of seven or eight feet, so as to afford a clear area of six feet at least in height after the arrangements intended there shall have been completed, and it being determined to introduce a powerful heater with the view of warming the passage and several of the principal apartments, a supply of fresh air should be provided below as indicated around the heating apparatus, *a*, in the basement, Fig. 76.

A second general supply can be given above by one or more of the windows in the upper passage when the state of the external air is not objectionable.

The heater is arranged so as to admit of its being supplied with air from the passage principally, as in the preceding case, Fig. 73, when the introduction of a little fresh air is sufficient.

For the removal of vitiated air, in addition to the usual resources by doors and windows, a special flue is placed next the kitchen, and the instructions being that it should have the power of acting on the dining-room, the parlor, two bed-rooms as well as the passages, the kitchen, cellars and closets, the principal connections are indicated accordingly.

All the individual rooms being provided with internal windows, when these are in operation, vitiated air from the

upper part of the passage can be discharged by the ventilating
flues, V and W, or by opening the upper part of the windows
in this passage, on any occasion when the general ventilating
flue may not be in action.

The plan of the principal floor, Fig. 74, shows an entrance
hall or vestibule, *A*, communicating with the apartments on
either side by large sliding doors, each in two parts, that are
hung so as to be moved with extreme facility. When both
parts are open, they afford with the parlor, *B*, and the dining-
room, *C*, accommodation for a number of persons. Glazed
doors, freely perforated above and below, are placed at *D*. *E*
is a bed-room, and *F* the kitchen with the ventilating shaft
which is attended to there, and always heated by the flues
from the kitchen fire-place, whether the special fire-place
provided for it shall be in use or not. Two closets near the
back entrance are provided with flues proceeding to the
lateral ventilating shaft that is indicated in the section, along
with others immediately above them.

The large ingress for fresh air tinted red in *a* permits the
whole stair-case and vestibule to have the advantage of the
rotatory currents described under " stairs," Fig. 78, when there
are few persons present, or supplies fresh warm air solely by a
direct ascent when a crowd is in attendance.

The central apparatus below warms the whole house through
the stairs, besides conveying special currents on either side to
the dining-room, parlor, and contiguous bed-room. A small
steam apparatus used principally in the kitchen for cooking,
conveys steam to the steam bath G, on the floor above, and also
to steam plates or radiators in the bed-rooms H, I, K. The
other bed rooms, M, N, L, have fire-places, and E, on the first
floor, has a supply of warm air from the heater as well as a fire-

place. The upper passage is warmed by the air ascending from A.

The diagrammatic section indicates the shaft S, with its descending supply T, and the two principal divisions V and W, which receive air directly or by branches from all the rooms, passages, and closets. The dotted blue lines indicate the progress of the flues from the ceiling of the different floors on which they appear.

The kitchen and basement communicate directly with the shaft.

In the bath room any amount of warm air and steam can be given at G, and the ventilating apertures are larger, but, like the rest, under the control of valves.

Though the house can be heated by the heater alone, without steam or open fires, still in this instance a preference is given to all the arrangements shown, the heater below being used alone on ordinary occasions. The steam apparatus is put in operation in extreme weather and when a steam bath is required; and the open fires are not generally necessary, though available according to the desire of those who occupy the apartments in which they are placed.

CHAPTER XXVII.

VENTILATION OF THE PRINCIPAL APARTMENTS IN A HOUSE WHERE
LARGE PARTIES ARE GIVEN.

In a house where large assemblies are held, and the principal rooms are brilliantly illuminated with gas, the air presents the usual characters at a party said to be crowded to suffocation. If fresh air be given by the windows in cold weather, the impression it produces on such occasions is so intolerable, when the constitution has been subjected for a short time to the over heated atmosphere, that it cannot be borne by those in the vicinity. If warm air be admitted, its temperature is so great, and quantity so small, that the result is unsatisfactory. Farther, a damp basement and a kitchen below give abundant proof in the principal apartment of the source from which they are supplied with air, whenever the heating apparatus is in use. The proprietor determines to correct these evils, for which the following measures are requisite.

The right adjustment of the drains and the control and removal of vitiated and offensive damp air from the basement, *a*, Fig. 77. Part of the floor requires to be raised under any circumstances, so as to secure the formation of a proper channel for the supply of air to the warming apparatus.

The enlargement and reconstruction of the channel for the supply of air, *b*, and of the brick-work around the heater, *c*, in the manner explained in the pages on houses, stairs, &c.

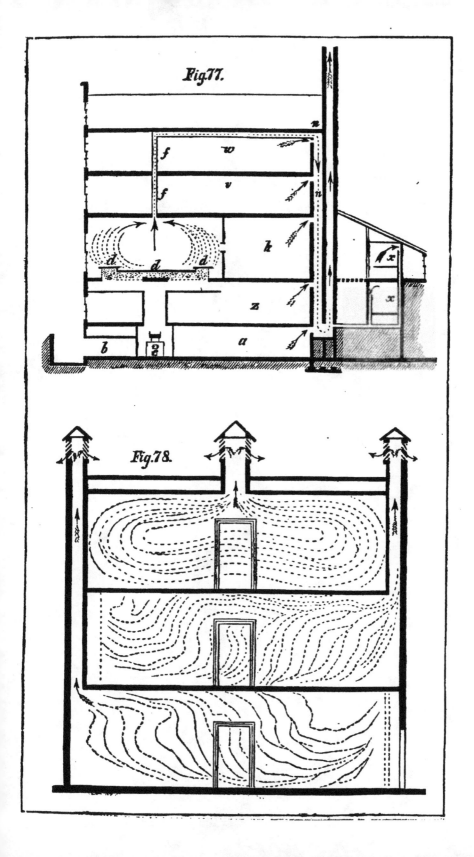

Fig. 77.

Fig. 78.

The formation of the largest openings practicable for the supply and distribution of a milder atmosphere to the principal apartment, $d\ d\ d$, at the skirting and fire-places (not used when the rooms are crowded) and wherever an ingress can be given without interfering with the use of the floor, as at every part of the base-board. The construction of internal windows above the doors leading from the entrance to the principal apartments. The direct removal of the products of the combustion of gas from the highest part of the ceiling, by a special flue, f, which, in the case under consideration, can be formed solely in the position indicated, unless with great inconvenience to existing arrangements.

The construction of a ventilating flue, m, and of a descending branch, n, to ventilate the principal apartments, d and k, advantage being taken at the same time of the opportunity of ventilating the apartments, w, v, z, and the closets, $x\ x$.

CHAPTER XXVIII.

TEMPORARY VENTILATION OF LARGE ROOMS IN AN OLD HOUSE WHERE
NUMBERS ARE CROWDED FOR A SHORT PERIOD DURING SEVERE
WEATHER.

AN old house, Fig. 78, is to be used temporarily for lodging as
great a number of laborers for a few weeks as can be accommodated on straw mattresses placed on the floor; a space not
more than three feet by eight can be allowed for each man.
There is no provision whatever for ventilation except by doors
and windows, and the air from the stairs and passages, except
in the upper floor, is too bad to be used. What course should
be adopted in respect to the ventilation, there being neither
time nor means for anything but the simplest arrangements?
Cut through the upper floors and the roof so as to form the
three vitiated air flues that are seen terminating immediately
above the roof; about the distance of two feet from the doors or
windows, put up a screen of gauze, or partitions made of any
porous cloth, so as to permit the air to pass with as gentle and
extended a flow as possible, and with a much less impulse than
might otherwise be experienced by those nearest to the windows. Regulate the entrance and egress of air by a valve on
the discharge flue, and by the ingress also, if the wind be powerful, or the current very strong and cold. If the air can by any
simple arrangements be received first in a proper condition in
the passage, it may then be permitted to enter by the doors, as

exemplified in the upper floor, giving a more gentle impulse in severe weather by the increased diffusion thus available, and by being tempered more or less in the passage.

This matter should be made the subject of careful examination, as sometimes the closing of an aperture connected with a drain, a sewer, or some damp basement, may at once relieve the air in the stairs from all objections, and admit the free use of a large entrance, stair-case and passages, instead of taking air solely and directly from the external atmosphere by the window.

There is nothing more dangerous than a strong local draught of air playing continuously in the same direction upon the face and throat, especially when the constitution has been so fatigued and exhausted as not to be readily aroused to its excessive action. Whoever ventilates should consider it a part of his duty, to guard against excessive draughts.

In a large bed-room, and with the bed at a distance from the window, or with appropriate curtains, there is no danger from a small portion of a window being open at night. In the more crowded habitations of the extreme poor, without diffusion, it is often highly dangerous to those in the vicinity.

CHAPTER XXIX.

VENTILATION OF HOTELS.—NOTES IN REFERENCE TO THE NATIONAL
HOTEL DISEASE AT WASHINGTON.

In the largest mansions, palatial structures and hotels, opportunities occur for treating them to some extent in the same manner as public buildings, more especially the dining room, the ball room, or any apartment appropriated for public meetings or other assemblies. As it is not intended, however, that these pages should include the consideration of public buildings, it will be sufficient here to give an outline of some points not so specially mentioned hitherto, and to state that though a central ventilating power is generally the most desirable in individual buildings, cases constantly occur where it may not be an object to effect the most extensive centralization practicable, and in which therefore a few independent shafts or ventilating turrets may be advantageously introduced as a substitute.

There are also many instances where an engine may be used instead of shafts as a moving power for forced or systematic ventilation, though apertures for discharge should always be provided under any circumstances. Without these, vitiated air may often be driven from one room to another and not be discharged at a proper place, or it may even recoil in one portion of an apartment, while fresh air is ascending in another.

It cannot be too strongly represented, that the greater the

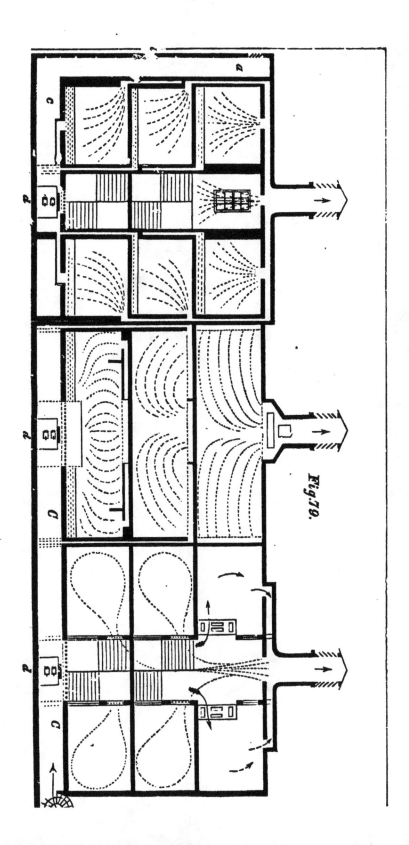

Fig.79.

number of rooms, halls, and passages in any building, the greater the annoyance from vitiated air or from local and offensive currents, if a sufficient supply of air be not provided, and a well organized escape for the vitiated air.

Further, the greatest perfection in ventilation is always accompanied by an ingress and egress, or supply and discharge, so balanced that there is no objectionable current at doors. If an objectionable current move outwards, then the supply forced in by the external air or by any instrument used for this purpose, must be too great, unless the discharge of the vitiated air be too small. On the other hand, if the offensive current proceeds inwards, then the supply of external air must be too small, or the action of the shaft or channel by which the vitiated air is discharged too great.

A little reflection on these two examples will simplify many cases that are apt to be very perplexing to those unaccustomed to enter on such questions. Nor is it possible in complicated buildings such as large hotels, always to avoid such difficulties, where they have been built without regard to systematic ventilation.

There are four evils, however, to which many hotels are peculiarly subject, that can be entirely avoided with proper attention to them.

1. The accumulation of vitiated air in the public apartments, arising from the ineffective discharge of the products of respiration, of the combustion of gas, and from the presence of excessive moisture, or vitiated air in the refreshment rooms.

2. The prevalence of tobacco-smoke, an evil from which many hotels are remarkably free.

For the entire and absolute control of the vitiated air from smoking rooms, a ventilating flue should be made to withdraw the smoke so that it cannot enter into any passages, stairs, or other apartments where its use is not allowed.

3. Emanations from kitchens and sculleries.

Without a proper ventilating arrangement these can never be entirely excluded.   Even if placed in external buildings the wind may drift them upon the hotel.

4. Vitiated air from closets, drains and sewers.

The control and absolute exclusion of all vitiated air from these sources is equally indispensable to health and comfort.

The noted case of the National Hotel at Washington, where so many hundreds suffered very lately, was not unconnected with the condition of the ventilation.   Whether other causes contributed or not, is a question that is not entered on here ; recent facts and statements that have been made on this point may leave this an open question till the whole of the evidence on the subject shall be published and compared, but in the mean time personal observations in this Hotel at the time referred to gave proof that there was, in one part of the hotel at least, a discharge of vitiated air from drains of so intense a character that it produced instantaneous vomiting on some occasions, and affected numbers in a less degree at the moment, who were nevertheless attacked at a subsequent period.

The report of the chairman of the Board of Health at Washington, Dr. King Stone, as well as the report of the Committee of the Academy of Medicine of New York on this subject, fully express the conviction of the important effect produced by the emanations from the drains, and attribute the National Hotel Disease to this cause.   No other cause has as yet been proved to have been in operation, and even if it were, it would in no way alter the conviction entertained, that the emanations from the drains constituted an evil of great magnitude, and capable of producing the most disastrous results.

Let it be recollected that there are no deleterious gases that can arise from the admixture of chemicals that may meet in obstructed drains and sewers, that may not find their way into hotels, houses, and other buildings, as well as the products of putrefaction from animal and vegetable matters. Sewers may discharge there the products found at the distance of miles, particularly if they be trapped so as to exclude the access of air in the streets. And who can estimate the emanations that may not proceed from such sources when they arise from chemicals discharged from a manufactory, an apothecary's store, a paint shop, a telegraph office, or the poisoned remains of animals that may have accumulated in the sewers? Further the very cement or mortar may imbibe materials that discharge sulphureted or arseniureted hydrogen from compound mixtures on fermentation, or from the action of an acid; and these find their way by a retrograde current in the drains and sewers to any building connected with them where the drains have been injured, and the traps rendered ineffective.

Lastly, it should not be forgotten that if one or two hundred thousand dollars be the probable amount of loss to the individual sufferers and proprietors, the whole of this sum might probably have been saved, to say nothing of loss of life, and loss of occupation to numbers interested, had the hotel been ventilated as had been suggested during the preceding year, and again recommended before the disease there assumed such a condition that the medical authorities deemed it indispensable that it should be closed. Even one or two hundred dollars would have removed the worst evils arising from the drains at the moment, by discharging the gaseous products from them by an independent channel, till the greater and general evil proceeding from obstructed sewers could have been removed. Can a more striking example be found of the importance of Hygiene and the chemistry of daily life being made subjects of elementary study in all schools public or private? Those most largely interested were not impressed with the importance of the ventilation previously recommended, till it was too late to attempt to keep the hotel open longer at the period mentioned.

The improvement of numerous hotels has been very marked in recent years in the great majority of modern cities, but an instance such as the National Hotel at Washington has presented, and the results of the inquiries instituted on this subject, point out emphatically how much is yet to be done in improving the Hygiene of cities as well as of individual habitations. Nor have such inquiries a local importance alone; it would be difficult to select any cities without finding some hotels presenting parallel evils arising from drains and sewers, however inferior generally in point of intensity.

If the ordinary condition of the atmosphere at Paris be examined, of the air on the banks of the Thames at London, or over a large portion of Berlin, abundant evidence will be obtained of the effect of causes that have been increasing for ages in deteriorating the atmosphere of these capitals. The most Herculean labors, as well as the expenditure of millions, can alone place them in that position which, with the aid of public opinion and of parliamentary and municipal authority, they may at last attain.

———

There are few remarks in the preceding chapters that do not apply to hotels as well as other buildings, particularly those on ventilating shafts, lighting, heating, and cooling, and the details as to the ingress and egress of air at entrances, passages, stairs, and individual apartments.

The accompanying Fig. 79 explains the general suite of arrangements which it is desirable to introduce in crowded hotels. Air from the least objectionable source is conveyed by one or two channels, *a* and *b*, to general reservoirs or distributing chambers, *c*, *c*. Steam, stove, or hot-water apparatus, *d*, *d*, *d*, gives heat there, particularly to the large central apartments indicated by the flues on the left proceeding to them.

Some of the apartments on the right, not admitting the introduction of specific flues, are provided with internal windows that enable each room to be supplied from the staircase, and also to discharge vitiated air into it. Two rooms above them receive air by the door, and discharge vitiated air directly by the ceiling.

In the large central apartments that are approached by corridors looking into the interior of an open quadrangle, great diffusion is given to the entering air, as they are often very crowded, and it is therefore necessary that the influx of the air, though well warmed, should be mild and gentle. The rest of the building is ventilated by a shaft similar to that shown by Fig. 10, constructed principally to control the atmosphere of the basement, the kitchen, closets, and a few apartments in the vicinity.

The bed-rooms generally have not received any special ventilation. All are provided with fire-places.

In building a new hotel, every apartment whatsoever can easily have some ventilation introduced, when the whole arrangements are placed on a uniform system. In existing hotels where the ventilation is defective, the great object is in general to supply the passages with a proper atmosphere, and remove the vitiated air and emanations from gas lights in these passages and in individual rooms.

In hotels the introduction of machinery for the movement of air is not necessary, though there are many cases where an engine is maintained in action for pumping water and other purposes where it could often be used advantageously. In such instances, the fanner is usually made to force fresh air into a larger channel as indicated on the right in Fig. 79, branches from this source being distributed to passages and individual apartments as illustrated in Fig. 80.

In using a fanner, the diffusion given in crowded apartments should be still more carefully carried out than where a ventilating shaft is used, though desirable in all cases in proportion to the numbers likely to crowd upon a given area. In Fig. 79, in the central portion, and on the left, various modes of giving diffusion are shown; according to these the air enters principally at the side, or at the ceiling, so as not to encroach at all, or only as slightly as possible on the floor.

Fanners may be used in the same manner as shafts for the removal of vitiated air, instead of effecting this object by the propulsion of fresh air. But the propelling system is usually preferred, as it charges the ventilated apartment so fully with air, if placed in effective operation, that the excess tends to prevent local draughts at doors and windows. Nevertheless, it is not considered desirable to omit the provision of a proper discharge for vitiated air, a point that is sometimes omitted where fanners are used, as it then is apt to recoil and produce a local annoyance wherever it may incline, if not discharged

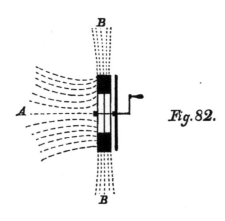

Fig. 82.

Fig. 81.

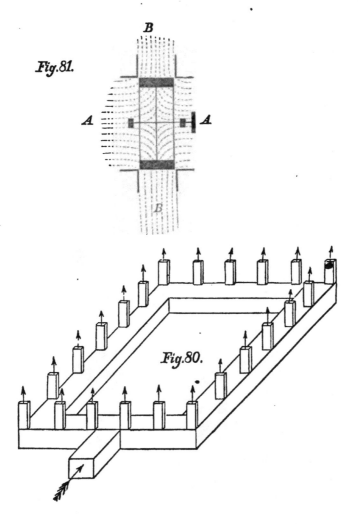

Fig. 80.

at a proper level, and in such a manner as not to contaminate the entering fresh air.

Fig. 81 indicates the movement of air to and from a fanner. It always approaches by the sides and is discharged in a stream by the blades whenever the extremities are left freely exposed. Placed in a case or large chamber where the entering and the discharged air are carefully kept apart, it will be obvious that if the apartment to be ventilated be connected by appropriate channels with A, either on one or both sides, air will be withdrawn from it, the external air having free access to it, and supplying fresh air to this apartment as the fanner continues in operation. But if AA be placed freely in connection with the open air, and B with the room to be ventilated, then fresh air will be propelled into this apartment.

The fanner is often supplied with air on one side only, as in Fig. 82, the currents produced in this manner being treated as in the preceding case.

There is perhaps no class of instruments in which greater improvements have been made in recent years than in these for the movement of air, particularly the fanner, the screw and the pump. Nevertheless, both in hotels and houses, it is recommended that the structure should be arranged, wherever it is practicable, to give adequate ventilation without them. Further, where they are used, instruments of great magnitude and moving with a low velocity, are preferable to those of a small size propelled with great velocity.

CHAPTER XXX.

TENEMENT HOUSES.

THE landlord of a tenement house finds that there is great complaint of cold and draught on the ground floor, of heat and bad air in the upper floors, and of an offensive atmosphere from the basement and cellars pervading the staircase generally, and obtaining access from it to the habitations on all the different floors. He knows also, that water comes in from the roof, injuring the upper floor on the breaking up of every frost, when snow has accumulated there, and desires to place the whole building in better condition.

The drainage of the basement requires attention in the first instance, where it is ascertained that it is subject to the infiltration of water at all times, particularly when the tide is full, and that the surface of the floor is perpetually damp. Nothing so effectually checks this evil as raising the level of the floor by filling it in with materials that set as a cement, covering the whole with some waxy, bitumnious, or asphaltic composition that has no objectionable odor, making the drainage good, and trapping the drain so as to exclude entirely any gaseous products from a neighboring sewer. It is better to leave a cellar with an altitude of six feet only, and a dry floor, than to have it damp, whatever be its height and the amount of accommodation it may afford.

Further, from the operations carried on in the basement, where there is a powerful stove and cooking apparatus acces-

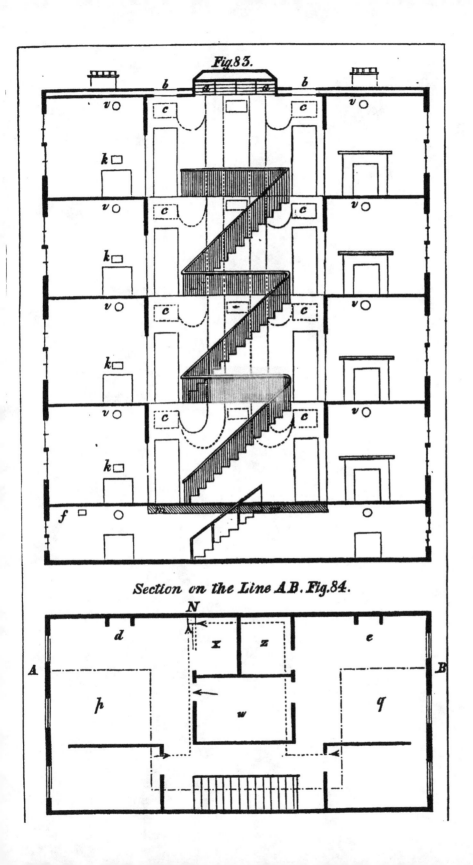

Fig. 83.

Section on the Line A.B. Fig. 84.

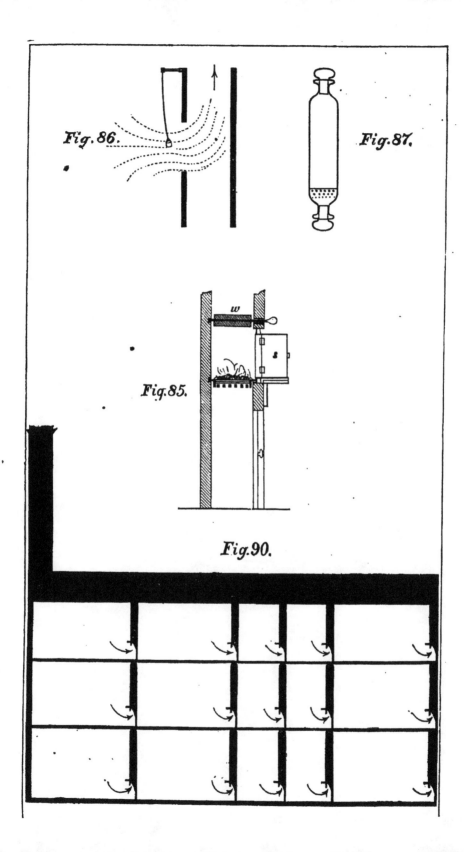

Fig. 86.

Fig. 87.

Fig. 85.

Fig. 90.

sible to all the families on the different floors, as well as a boiler, it is essential to have a special ventilating flue from the basement, f, Fig. 83, and to fix a board, m, m, about one foot deep, around the opening for the stairs, and at the level of the ceiling. This gives the flue, f, full power of action in carrying off bad air and vapors at the ceiling, before they descend below the level of the board at m; and so long as they are above this level, they cannot escape by the stairs.

One of the flues in the basement should be appropriated for this ventilation, or at all events an opening made into it, so that it can be used for this purpose, from time to time, and to any extent that circumstances may permit.

To remedy the other complaints, the following arrangements, or some modification of them, are desirable. The staircase has no supply of air whatever, when the doors below are shut, except the small amount that may enter by leakage there; but sixteen doors on the different floors, as well as the basement, may all draw more or less upon the passage and stairs when there are many fires kindled, and no windows opened for a supply in consequence of the state of the weather. The result is that one or more doors are opened on every floor to derive some benefit from the atmosphere in the staircase, and the lower floors discharge their vitiated air, which ascends and oppresses the occupants of the upper floors. Some of the chimneys overpower others, drawing down smoke which pervades the staircase. The occupants are forced in self-defence to shut their doors, and open their windows, till the cure becomes worse than the remedy, when they again return to their previous position, alternating between these opposite evils so long as they do not choose to suffer quietly the inconveniences that result from their unventilated dwellings.

The first step in remedying these defects should be to give more air to the staircase, and were the different families to be supplied with warm air in winter by a stove acting on the passage, and charged by the landlord on their rent, he would probably do more by this act to increase the comfort of his houses than by any other measure that could be mentioned. Nor would it be difficult to find parties who would undertake this for a small sum, and make a business of it. People in general don't want ventilation when they are cold or subject to shivering local currents. But there is no mode in which a series of habitations can so economically expend a portion of their fuel, as in warming their passages and staircases. The vertical sides of the skylight, a, a, Fig. 83, afford a good opportunity for the supply of air; it should enter through perforated zinc, to reduce its impetus, and valves should be provided that the apertures may be closed to any extent in extreme weather. One or two extra openings should also be made at b, b, for the discharge of vitiated air in summer, if extra ventilation be required; but any apertures made above, if large enough, will generally act both for the admission and discharge of air, and it is not desirable to have many valves to close in winter.

Again, to enable the different floors to partake more readily of the improved supply, the leakage at the doors should be increased by planing the doors slightly below and above, or apertures, c, c, c, &c., may be made above each door, and supplied with valves or louvres, which will enable them to act in the manner explained in describing " internal windows."

Entering now the individual habitations on the separate floors which are arranged on a plan very common in some parts of the United States, it will be found that they have no supply of air, except by doors or windows, nor any means of discharge except by these or the fire-place at d and e, Fig. 84, while two rooms, p, q, out of four have no fire-places, and one bed closet, w, has neither fire-place nor window, though provided with two doors. Two still smaller closets, x, z, or presses, are interposed between part of the principal rooms, one of which contains a water pipe and sink, the other being devoted to stores.

All rooms having fire-places, should, if the flues are suitable for this purpose, be pierced immediately under the ceiling, and an aperture, v, made square or circular and from four to six inches in diameter, or as near that as the structure and size of the bricks may render most desirable. This can be used on all occasions for the discharge of vitiated air from the ceiling, when the state of the fire and the external weather permits, and every facility should be given to promote its action by a proper top or cap where it communicates with the external air, so that it may be used as frequently as possible when wanted, even if no fire be in use. Further, an adjusting valve should be adapted to it, so as to regulate the amount of discharge most suitable at any particular period, or one of the Arnott balance valves usually sold by stove dealers, may be used, where there is a tendency to the return of smoke.

None of these arrangements, however, give the power to each tenement to secure the active ventilation of a single room in sultry and oppressive summer weather, when an ordinary fire cannot be used, or in a case of fever or other infectious disease, that causes apprehension to the families on every floor.

Even if no resources for these purposes be provided, the tenement house will be greatly improved by the measures mentioned. But a further improvement is still desirable, the introduction of a special ventilating flue, or the modification of one of the fire-places so as to admit of its being used on all or any of the individual apartments on which it may be deemed right to give it the power of operating.

Many are deterred from entertaining such a proposition in consequence of the presumed difficulties, but an examination of the examples given in respect to such rooms, will show that this object may be secured at any time for a temporary purpose by the use of the fire-places d or e.

In constructing a new house, however, or altering that under consideration, it would be advisable to remove entirely the partition that is indicated at one of the presses x (by dotted lines), and to construct there a special ventilating flue, in every tenement, carrying from it two tubes, from four to six inches in diameter, according to the course indicated, and by these a ventilating power could be brought to bear on any of the rooms, bed-rooms, or closets.

This flue might be constructed in such a manner as to be available for many minor operations, where a very small fire, a lamp, or a gas burner would give all the requisite heat, though the fire-place provided for actual ventilation should be as powerful, to meet extreme cases, as can be safely used with the ventilating flue.

During warm and sultry weather, the defective ventilation of tenement houses is often greatly aggravated by the want of some small and inclosed fire that can give the little heat required from time to time, at such periods, by numerous families, where the whole habitation is incommoded by the use of the winter stove, if it be resorted to, or much time and fuel lost in using a small portable open fire-place by the currents of air that dash over it, and cool anything that is placed upon it, sometimes almost as rapidly as it is heated. It is a great convenience in such instances, to have the chimney-piece of the apartment used as a kitchen, made of iron, and placed as low as the opening required at the fire-place will permit, and to have a small portable grate made with light iron, and fitting the interior of the flue at the part indicated at *k*, Fig. 83. A close-fitting iron door is provided in front at *s*, Fig. 85, and a valve above at *w*. With such a resource many minor culinary operations can be conducted, warm air kept in contact with anything placed above the fuel, and all cooling or heating currents regulated by the valve on damper *w*, while from the position of the fires little heat, comparatively, escapes into the apartment; any amount of protection can be given by non-conductors within the door *s*.

In all such tenements, a small space should be cut off some of the apartments for a closet, whatever other arrangements may be made outside for general use. Without this, trifling cases of disease often become serious, and perhaps few circumstances give rise more frequently to disease than the want of proper attention to this subject in the construction of the humbler class of dwellings. The general remarks accordingly made in reference to drains and closets should form a very special subject of study among the proprietors and occupiers of tenement houses.

As to the periodical injury to the roof whenever a frost breaks up, it is in general greatly aggravated by the rain pipe being filled with water in many places and frozen so that there is no regular escape for water as the snow begins to melt. The water accordingly accumulates above and often depresses, by its great weight, the centre of the roof, which is never thoroughly drained again till the levels are altered.

An iron pipe introduced in the rain water pipe, through which steam can be made to pass from a boiler or kettle put on a fire-place in the upper floor, whenever there is an indication of an approaching thaw, will always keep the channel clear, and save much expense and annoyance.

Few circumstances contribute more to the improvement of the condition of the atmosphere in tenements and other places where it has at last produced effects that have been severely felt, than the introduction of simple tests for indicating the progress of currents of air, and the quality of air that has been greatly deteriorated. For these purposes, a thread, or a small cylinder of paper suspended by a thread, Fig. 86, may be placed before a ventilating aperture as an "indicator" to point out the progress of a current, and whether a back draught does not take place from time to time introducing noxious gases.

Again, if a phial be filled with lime water, and nine tenths of it be poured out while it is held in such a position that expired air from the operator does not gain direct access to it, then on corking it, and agitating freely the remaining tenth with the air that has entered, there will be a white precipitate of carbonate of lime, in proportion to the amount of carbonic acid in the air. A few trials will teach the operator the appearance he may expect with good air, which contains only a very minute amount of carbonic acid, and with air too largely charged with it. For more precise action instruments termed carbonometers are used, that give the effect of a measured quantity of air on the lime water.

A tubular phial, Fig. 87, having a stopple at either end is more convenient than an ordinary phial for common use. Holding it in an inclined position with the upper stopple out, the lime water is allowed to escape by the lower aperture, till a sufficient quantity has been removed. Both stopples are then restored and the phial agitated to show the result.

The phial is cleaned by water and a few drops of acid for a new experiment, washing away the acid completely by the free use of water.

It would be a great mistake were it supposed that air is always good where it gives no indication of any excess of carbonic acid. It is true that in the great majority of cases within doors its presence in undue proportion indicates generally the presence of other sources of a vitiated atmosphere, particularly excessive moisture, smoke, and animal exhalations. The test for carbonic acid gives no indications of the whole tribe of malarious impurities that are so powerful in the production of disease, nor of many other deleterious gases and vapors.

CHAPTER XXXI.

IMPROVEMENT OF BUILDINGS IN DENSELY POPULATED DISTRICTS.

IN carrying out a series of improvements in the construction of buildings in the most densely populated part of a large city, it is desired to replace very inferior and dilapidated tenements by large and well built dwelling-houses for a class of society where each family cannot afford to occupy more than a few rooms, to give the same facilities as are at present available for miscellaneous trades and occupations, and to introduce all improvements that will render these dwellings acceptable among those for whom they are intended, without adding to the rents. It is also desired to give ample space for free and airy streets, and, if possible, to secure a small open plot for the exercise and recreation of children, and for a school, the additional accommodation provided by the more elevated buildings to be erected, giving an opportunity of carrying all these objects into effect.

Few questions attract more attention on both sides of the Atlantic than those involved in such enterprises, and many are the details of improvement that have been suggested and carried into execution. Among these, warming, lighting and ventilating have generally been included, with increased facilities for the supply of water, drainage and cleansing. The substitution of incombustible materials for wood as largely as possible, and the charging of the latter with chemicals, to render it less combustible and less subject to dry rot, or the harboring of

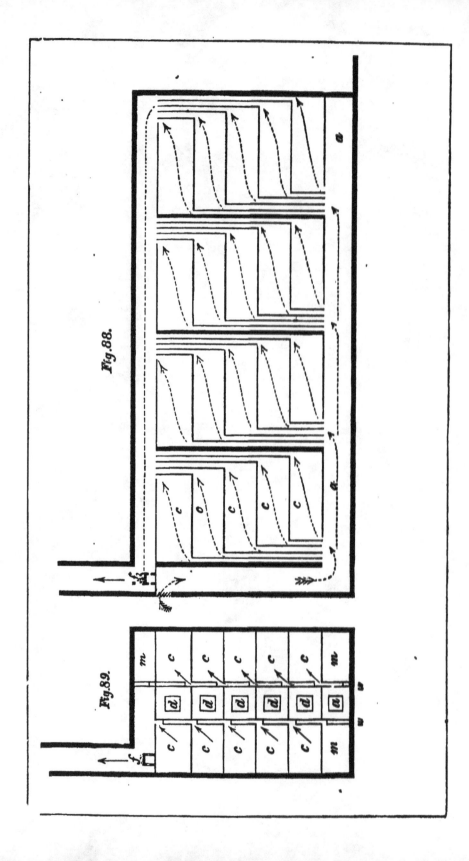

Fig.88.

Fig.89.

insects, has been another field of improvement. Stairs, window sashes, shelving, and beams or joists, all made of iron and combined with brick arches, now replace much of the inflammable material that has so long been in the ascendant. Glass, porcelain and glazed bricks, for the exclusion of moisture, are much employed in many places. And even tables, chairs and beds, long formed with great advantage of metal for some establishments, are in general use.

The great object is to combine the opportunities of economy which such an association of habitations necessarily presents with those improved arrangements in structure that have been developed in recent times, retaining all the individuality and privacy required in every separate dwelling.

These desiderata are attained with the greatest facility by the continental European system of living in flats or floors, where a very few rooms only are occupied by each family, one that has been long prevalent in Scotland also, from its more especial association with France in former times, though till lately more rarely introduced into England. All the later experiments, both in the United States and in Europe on this subject, appear to hold out this as one of the greatest sources of economy and improvement that can be introduced in populous cities pressed for space, and altogether overcrowded in many particular districts.

In the supply of pure air,—

The removal of vitiated air,—

The general communication of heat,—

The attendance and management of the entrance door, stairs, and passages,—

The supply of steam to every habitation,—

The supply of gas,—

The construction of closets,—

The right adjustment of drains,—

The provision of flues for the descent of dry ashes, sweepings, and all similar refuse,—and in many other improvements, buildings such as those contemplated can largely participate, while individual dwellings constructed without reference to others cannot have the same advantages except at a greatly increased expense.

Let it not be supposed that there is any intention to undervalue the many advantages that attend the construction of habitations where the proprietor or tenant claims everything above and below his dwelling as his own, as far as ever he can reach or penetrate. That is not the question. But how many are the tenements in which there are at least numerous deficiencies accompánied often by great discomfort, loss of health, and death, where the system advocated may bring ultimately, within the reach of all, habitations greatly superior to those at present in occupation, and which the inmates cannot expect to attain in any other way?

Let the accompanying Figs. 88, 89, exemplify the disposition of the leading chambers and flues for heating, cooling, and ventilating, and it will be seen with how much simplicity and economy a series of habitations might be supplied with warm or cool air from a common source, discharge vitiated air individually into a ventilating chamber provided for all, receive a steam pipe that would give them in an instant any heating surface they might require, and a boiling temperature to any liquid they might desire to heat, while windows and open fireplaces are as available to them as in any ordinary habitation. Further, if desired, all fire-places may be conveyed into a single ventilating turret, or into the vitiated air shaft, and the wholo of the roof be left available for use, or planked as a general resort in the cool of the evening, where the view, the climate, and the time of year render such opportunities grateful and agreeable, without being subject every moment to offensive products of combustion from a kitchen or any other fire-place.

Fig. 90 illustrates an arrangement of fire-flues that has been executed, a large horizontal flue receiving a series of flues from different floors, and discharging the products that pass through them by a single shaft. It is not recommended, however, that such flues should be introduced except where the system adopted can be properly sustained and controlled under one direction, and the draught of the shaft started or assisted by a fire at f, on all necessary occasions.

The diagrams, 88, 89 and 90, illustrate plans accordingly that cannot be completely and satisfactorily carried out unless they are controlled and managed in the same manner, to some extent at least, as public buildings similarly constructed. Much must depend on the details in individual buildings. Where a shaft can always be maintained at a moderate elevation of temperature sufficient to command a draught by the waste heat from any kitchen, boiler, or other fire-place, a concentration or union of flues effected with the view of leaving a roof entirely free from smoke is in many places so highly prized that it will always be viewed as an object of importance.

In the transverse section, Fig. 89, to which the same figures apply as in the general section, Fig. 88 a, is the fresh air and heating chamber supplied with air from some altitude, the quality of the air at a lower level being indifferent; b, the vitiated air chamber in the roof; c, c, c, &c., individual rooms or spaces that can be converted into a series of rooms; d, open corridors and a large window at the end of each corridor or passage; *w*, *w*, the walls by which tempered warm air is given to flues in each room according to the season of the year, the vitiated air flues being placed in the upper part of the same walls. *f*, the furnace, to be used when requisite for the ventilation.

m, *m*, the boiler room, and other places used as cellars, closets, and store rooms appropriated to the different habitations.

Every individual crowded locality should be carefully studied in reference to the sanitary improvements of which it appears to be most susceptible, or to stand in the greatest want. In some places cleansing is the great desideratum; in others, better drainage, closets, and a good supply of water. In another series of habitations no fair prospect of any permanent improvement can be held out till causes of a moral and social complexion shall have been the subject of attention.

CHAPTER XXXII.

EXTERNAL VENTILATION.

THE question of external ventilation—that is, the preservation of a pure atmosphere without a building, from which it may obtain an unobjectionable supply of air—is no less important than ventilation within doors. It may not be to the same extent under control, but external air often exerts an extreme influence, capable of producing the worst effects. Many circumstances connected with the condition of the air may be as entirely beyond the control of man as the quarter from which the wind blows. Others again are as much within his power as the system of ventilation adopted in individual dwellings. If the surface drainage and external cleansing be indifferent, impurities may arise indefinitely from such sources. If the house drainage and sewerage be imperfect, evils of equal magnitude may ensue. All collections of stagnant water loaded with animal and vegetable debris are deleterious. The vegetation of special plants, as some water-lilies, and the presence of fish, contribute to purify many waters. In some valleys without any natural opening, the atmosphere would become pestilential were it not for the purifying influence of vegetation.

Again, the materials used in different manufactories, the processes conducted there, and even the amount of smoke discharged in some cases, produce a most injurious effect upon the atmosphere of many habitations.

The system of building adopted may in itself be prejudicial and require alteration. A block of land, surrounded on every side by lofty buildings, has, in a stagnant atmosphere, a very indifferent supply of air; and if there should be any sources of nuisance within the block, the air from them, particularly when the barometer falls, is apt to pervade the whole area. Many places also, even though not surrounded on every side, have no sufficient openings from side to side, or end to end, to admit of an adequate circulation of air.

Lastly, the position of the district in respect to hill and dale, land and water, and the soil or foundation on which the building rests, and all circumstances connected with any local, geological peculiarity, or variety of climate, should be taken into consideration. In a valley where the prevailing winds sweep across the top of the rising ground on either side, buildings below are often subject to excessive heat and moisture. On isolated hills the air is scarcely ever in equilibrio; perpetual changes ensue; air is constantly drifting from side to side; heavy gases and vapors descend, while those that are light escape upwards. In the valley, the great object is to excite ventilation and remove stagnant, vitiated air. On the hill— to secure protection from its natural but excessive operation.

Again, if two houses exactly similar to each other be built, and the one be founded on gravel, and the other on a bed of granite, surrounded on every side by materials of the same kind, it will be obvious that rain and moisture will be removed rapidly by the gravel, while, without artificial drainage very carefully provided, it will stagnate on the granite foundation. The same is observed in districts abounding in clay, and in all places below any water line in the vicinity.

Further, even in open porous ground, where gravel may

predominate, if the overflow or waste from any large cesspool shall not be sufficiently washed away and diluted by the natural waters of the district and the artificial supply by which they are assisted, the whole ground near it will become saturated to an extent that must injuriously affect the atmosphere.

Cesspools should, accordingly, be very cautiously extended, lest they should eventually be the source of malaria, and ultimately contaminate streams of water which it may be important to preserve from such impurities.

All collections of stagnant water, in the immediate vicinity of houses, that cannot be directly removed by drainage, should be treated with quicklime, added from time to time till they lose their noxious qualities.

From these observations, the more prominent points will become apparent, that should engage attention in examining the locality in which it may be intended to build or select a house. Nothing, however, should be examined more carefully than the influence of the prevailing winds in conveying vitiated air from any marsh or manufactory, and the power which the proprietor may have in preventing any noxious works from being established in the vicinity, or enforcing them at least to be so conducted as to prevent any annoyance to those without, by processes similar to those explained in reference to the decomposition of noxious emanations.

In offices or individual apartments hemmed in on every side by tall buildings, the air is sometimes very good, at other times loaded with emanations from cellars and drains below or chimneys above. Products of combustion, visible or invisible, are sometimes blown down on one side of a court, affecting all air supplied by the windows on that side, and giving rise to long

8

continued headache or dyspeptic symptoms that give way with a change of dwelling.

The influence of stagnant pools and marshes on the atmosphere is well known, but the insidious effects of manufactories discharging vitiated air among a dense population, have not received a proportionate attention; nor are the manufacturers themselves always aware of it, as the fumes, gases and vapors are often less concentrated upon the workmen, however dense in chemical chambers and chimneys, than upon any house in the vicinity. It is vain for them in such cases to appeal to the health of the workmen. In other instances, those engaged in the factory are the first to suffer from the atmosphere developed in it.

The effect of vitiated air from graveyards does not require so much attention as in former times, as the almost universal recognition of the principle that intra-mural interments ought no longer to be permitted, has reduced one of the greatest evils that often preyed with extreme severity on populous cities. There appears still, however, to be a necessity for improvement in many individual localities. Old burial grounds within populous districts, though no longer used for new interments, should be freely and repeatedly sprinkled with quicklime, wherever offensive emanations are manifest on a fall of the barometer. In some new burial grounds, the use of a few lime shells at every burial, is desirable. In all, the most vigorous and active vegetation should be sustained on the surface, as the most pleasing and available means of absorbing noxious gases and vapors, and preventing the formation of a malarious district, prone to convey its evil influence even to the distance of miles, in particular conditions of the atmosphere.

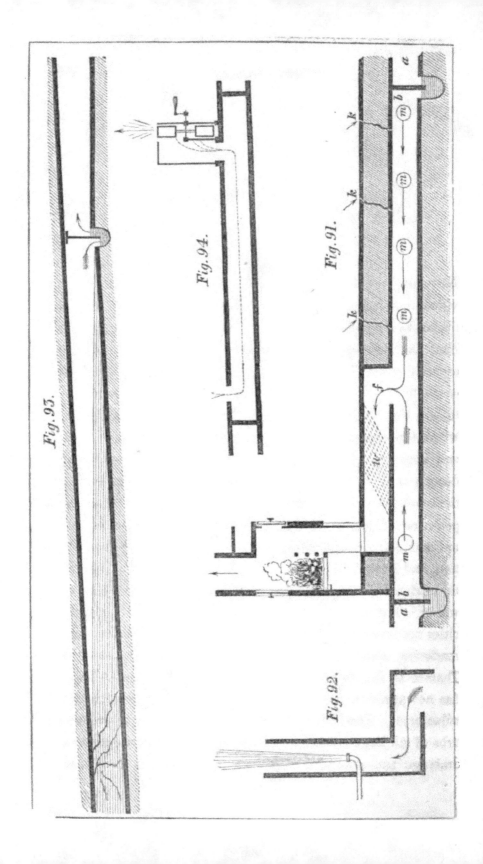

Fig. 95.

Fig. 94.

Fig. 91.

Fig. 92.

CHAPTER XXXIII.

DRAINS AND CLOSETS.

No arrangements conduce more to comfort and health in individual habitations, than the right construction of the closets, drains, and sewers connected with them. The drains at the National Hotel at Washington, during the prevalence of the severe illness that recently took place there, presented a marked example of evils that are common both to town and country, to one side of the Atlantic and the other, and in all places where the warnings of the nostrils are habitually disregarded, and inadequate provision made for the effective removal of decomposing refuse. In London, after the experience of a thousand years, the magnitude of the evils arising from the pollution of the Thames has attracted so much attention that millions of pounds are to be expended in improving its condition, and counteracting the effects that have arisen from the unrestricted discharge of the contents of the sewers into its waters. But the condition of Paris, Berlin, and other large cities not provided with means of discharge by water, without rendering what is available still more intolerable than the Thames at London, a preeminence which the Seine, at least, has not attained, equally presents an important problem for adjustment. Further, the innumerable habitations in the suburbs of all large cities, and in country places, where extended drainage and sewerage, if it ever be introduced, cannot, at least for one or more generations, be expected to assume a systematic form, demand the most careful attention.

When the supply of water is adequate, and a proper system of drainage and sewerage in operation, the great desiderata in each habitation are the entire exclusion of air proceeding from drains and sewers, and the ventilation of individual closets.

If a leakage of bad air be manifest from any drain, which is not removed on flushing it with a copious stream of water, it should be carefully examined, repaired if any local defect be observed, and above all, its gaseous contents should be disconnected by a proper trap, from the sewer into which it leads. A sewer may discharge vitiated air into a drain that may pass into the house from which it proceeds, and the whole contents of the gaseous products from miles of sewerage may in certain cases be conveyed to an individual building.

When there is a leakage from any considerable portion of a drain, that cannot for some time be put in proper order, it is often desirable to place a ventilating power upon every portion within the habitation affected by it. Fig. 91 indicates a portion of a drain, *a a*, trapped at both extremities, and a ventilating flue, *f*, discharging vitiated air from it. By this flue it may be led to any fire-place where the products can be decomposed or rendered innocuous. Fresh air enters at all cracks, crevices, and other openings, *k k k*, that previously discharged vitiated air. Such a remedy applied at any hotel or other building gives immediate relief, the water traps, *b b*, permitting the free flow of the ordinary drainage, while they cut off on both sides all gaseous emanations, either from drains or sewers; *m m m m* indicate the various openings from the lesser drains proceeding from the building to that portion of the drain which is ventilated. Wire gauze is introduced at w, where the presence of combustible or explosive gases may be apprehended.

Fig. 92 shows a ventilating flue worked by steam which can be made to act on the drain in the same manner as the fire in Fig. 91. It has the disadvantage of not consuming the products, but does not require wire gauze where inflammable gases are evolved.

Large sewers should always be ventilated at special places, selected for the purpose, and shafts built for this object, when it is desirable to remove the vitiated air in them, and to prevent that extreme intensity of bad air being developed that is formed in an absolutely air-tight sewer. When frozen or otherwise obstructed, and not ventilated, deleterious gas may be forced through the water and under the traps, as in Fig. 93, rendering them entirely useless.

Again, in individual closets, within habitations, the usual mode of ventilating consists in opening a window. The result, however, is that vitiated air is often blown from the closet to the contiguous passage, and from that to the house, instead of being discharged externally.

Fig. 94 illustrates the removal of a dangerous atmosphere from a portion of a sewer by the action of a fanner previous to the workmen entering with the view of repairing it; *m m*, are temporary obstructions to the further ingress of bad air.

In any house having a special ventilating flue or shaft, one branch should be led to it from the closet; and then, on all occasions when the window is shut, vitiated air from the closet will be discharged by the ventilating flue. Air may pass from the passage to the closet, but none return from the closet to the passage, unless the window or door be too widely opened, and the draught to the passage strong.

The same practice ought to be adopted in reference to all cellars, individual apartments, cavities, or other spaces where vitiated air may be apt to accumulate.

Another point connected with this subject, of great practical importance, involves the whole question of the right adjustments for refuse in all places where there are no proper facilities for an extended system of drainage and sewerage, and where it is an object not to allow the material to run to waste.

The usual practice is the formation of large cesspools that are periodically cleansed, once or twice a year, and leave a mass of decomposing materials in a state of putrefactive fermentation throughout the whole year, except when frozen by the extreme cold of winter, as offensive to the nostrils as they are injurious to health, and prone too often to contaminate the ground in the vicinity with a perpetual malaria.

Every possible effort should be made to abate and alter such sources of nuisance and disease, and in many places of the indefinite multiplication of insects.

This subject assumes still greater importance when it is taken in conjunction with the fact that in many districts the pollution of the springs and streams is becoming so great, from the ordinary drainage and sewerage, that it has led to the inquiry for a remedy, equally applicable to the cesspool and to the common sewer.

How far new improvements may be realized, it is difficult to predict, but one point at least is manifest, that by draining off the liquid contents of such cesspools, by rendering them much smaller, by more frequent cleansing, and by the addition of various chemicals or other materials capable of absorbing moisture, the present system may be entirely altered, deprived of all its worst features, and the refuse converted into a dry, inodorous manure, the sale of which would at least compensate for the arrangement by which it is effected.

The number of trials that have been made of the system adverted to render it desirable that it should receive much more general attention, and that the agriculturist and the architect should lend their coöperation in carrying out an improvement that has been so warmly advocated, and which has already been partially carried into operation in many places. The removal, condensation, and absorption of moisture, forms the great feature of this plan. The materials then do not lose by fermentation; they become dry and inodorous; they are removed with little offence or objection; they become much more valuable as manures.

For such an object, accordingly, an iron tank, or other receptacle, should be so constructed as to be freely accessible on one side for the removal of refuse. This side, also made movable, should be next a door that can be opened so as to admit of a small cart being brought immediately under it whenever it is to be emptied. There should also be prepared a proper store of dried earth, burnt clay, ashes, turf, charcoal, powdered gypsum, green vitriol, or any other absorbents of moisture and of ammoniacal gas, such as can be conveniently obtained in each particular locality.

It is not presumed that arrangements for such purposes can be extensively introduced without some previous care and preparation in all populous districts where they may be most urgently required. But whenever the air is largely contaminated with the offensive cesspool, too much importance cannot be attached to the substitution of the dry closet, raised to a proper altitude, to admit of its being attended to with facility and economy. In numerous country places where it forms no part of the system adopted to convert such refuse entirely into fluid manure, the plan may in general be at once adopted.

But let it not be supposed that the very partial measure of merely connecting a cesspool with a drain or sewer can do much good. On the contrary, whatever advantages it may have in removing fluid contents, it is often accompanied by a still more intolerable atmosphere than before; the materials being more, though not sufficiently accessible to the air, become still more putrescent, if the drain or sewer be not carefully trapped. Further, vitiated air may now be added from an indefinite extent of drains or sewers. Such are too frequently the results of attempts at drainage without an adequate supply of water, and where the provisions are too imperfect either for a proper system of liquid drainage, or for the construction of dry closets by the means explained.

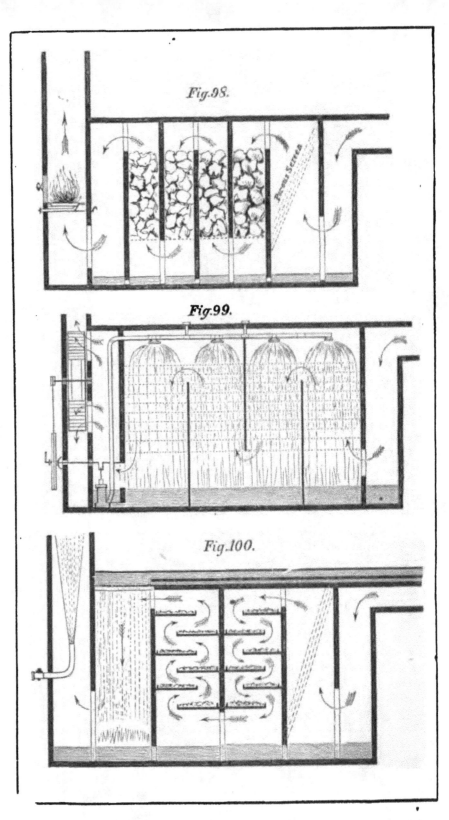

Fig.98.

Fig.99.

Fig.100.

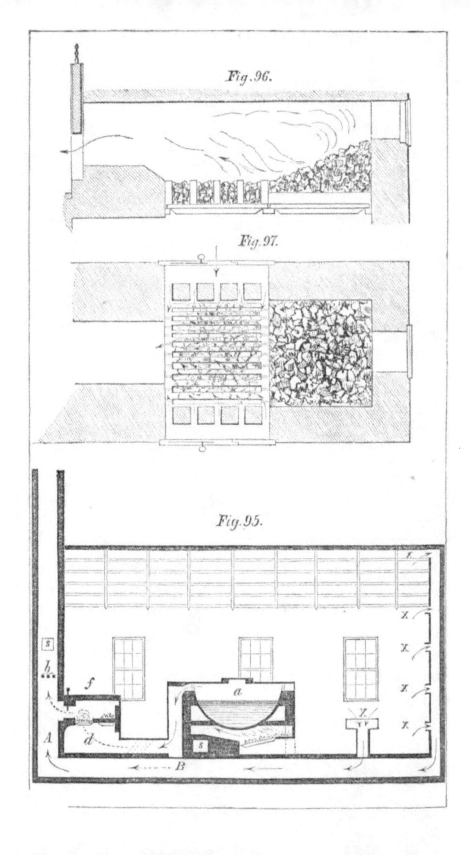

Fig. 96.

Fig. 97.

Fig. 95.

CHAPTER XXXIV.

DECOMPOSITION OF NOXIOUS GASES FROM MANUFACTORIES IN POPULOUS DISTRICTS.

A MANUFACTORY in the midst of a dense and populous district discharges offensive and deleterious gases and vapors. What resources are available for the prevention of just complaints, without resorting to the extreme measure of removing the manufactory from a site where numerous interests desire to retain it?

In crowded cities and populous districts, few causes are more frequently the source of great oppression than the discharge of vitiated air from manufactories where noxious products arise directly from the materials used, and the chemical agents mixed with them, or are formed during their decomposition by heat. The higher the temperature of the climate, the greater in general is the annoyance they give.

In some cases, it is attempted to remove the evil by lofty chimneys discharging the vitiated air at a considerable altitude. It is seldom, however, that the factory is so arranged as to prevent all noxious emanations escaping, except by such chimneys. And even when this is the case, they are prone to descend upon individual places with various winds and currents, so that there is no certainty of their removal.

The desire not to interfere with trade often induces many to submit to the offensive atmospheres thus produced, in the belief that no remedy but removal is available.

Difficulties often increase in dealing with such questions where the distinction is not made between those cases where a population rises around the factory, and others in which the factory is introduced among numbers in a locality previously free from such causes of offence. In the first case, the manufacturer has a claim to compensation, or to assistance from the neighboring district, if compelled to remove, or to alter his processes so as to remedy the subject of complaint.

In doing this it will greatly facilitate numerous adjustments if it be recollected that all emanations from animal and vegetable materials may be entirely consumed and decomposed by the combined action of heat and air, so as to be resolved into products of the same nature, and consequently not more objectionable, than those that proceed from the combustion of ordinary fuel. Further, all noxious gases and vapors, not altered in this manner by heat, may be decomposed, or absorbed by the action of chemicals, such as chlorine, lime, alkalies, acids, and other substances, according to the nature of the offensive products formed.

Fig. 95 points out the general arrangement of flues in a factory where many operations are carried on that evolve offensive products, decomposable by heat, but requiring different treatment, according to their several peculiarities, and the amount formed in a given time. a indicates a boiler evolving such products; b, a small fire acting on them in a shaft, when it is sufficient for the purpose; $d\ d$, the course they are made to take when the most powerful mode of decomposition by heat is necessary to give satisfaction: f, the furnace used on such occasions; A and B are valves regulating the course taken by different products, according as they merely discharge them into the shaft S, or force them previously through the decomposing furnace; *f x x x*, are apertures in various descending flues or channels, by which the vitiated air from other processes, or apartments with stoves, may be conveyed to the shaft with or without the use of the decomposing furnace.

Figs. 96 and 97 show more particularly a plan and section of the decomposing furnace. The large supply of fuel not resting on the furnace bars gives an abundance of red hot cinders at all times, and the fresh air passages, tinted red on either side of the furnace bars, permit a sufficiency of fresh air to maintain constantly all the bright fire requisite, when the transmitted vapors or gases are otherwise apt to extinguish the fire of the decomposing furnace.

When inflammable gases or vapors are disengaged, they are usually diluted largely with air before they are conveyed to the decomposing furnace, so as to diminish or avoid all risk of explosion, and made, as an additional security against the return of flame, to pass through several leaves or frames of wire gauze, very carefully fitted. Further special adaptations must be made to meet the peculiarities of individual cases.

In the three following Figs., 98, 99, 100, different modes are shown of subjecting the passing currents to the action of materials that absorb, condense, or decompose the impurities which it is desired to correct or remove.*

Fig. 98 indicates a ventilating shaft put in action by a fire, and drawing vitiated air through a condensing chamber, where masses of chalk and other chemicals absorb all the acid emanations evolved.

In Fig. 99 the ventilating power is a fanner, worked by a

---

* These and the three preceding figures are taken (slightly modified) from one of the reports drawn up by Dr. Reid, when engaged as one of the Commissioners for the health of towns in populous districts in England and Wales.

small engine which pumps at the same time the absorbing fluid and returns it constantly in the form of a shower of rain, till its action ceases, when a fresh charge is used.

The shower of artificial rain is often used as a moving power in the manner indicated in Fig. 100, where the counteracting agents are gaseous chemicals evolved from materials disengaged in broad plates, with upturned edges, like basins. Steam from a boiler aids the moving power, and may be used alone for this purpose.

Of these varied resources, none is so generally useful, or so easily available as the decomposing influence of heat. Cases can be pointed out where a single furnace has relieved a whole population from the most nauseous and offensive vapors, manifest, at times, at the distance of two or three miles, but totally imperceptible, even in contiguous habitations, when subjected to the action of an effective decomposing furnace.

THE END.

CPSIA information can be obtained
at www.ICGtesting.com
Printed in the USA
LVHW101348160422
716387LV00003B/232

9 783752 593495